Cha~~p~~---

The Birth of a Nation

I still remember that starry night in May 1948, a night when the shadow of uncertainty loomed heavily over our new homeland. Tel Aviv pulsed with an energy that was both electrifying and terrifying. The bustling streets were lined with Israeli flags fluttering proudly, symbols of renewed hope after years of suffering and perseverance. The Mossad intelligence center, discreetly nestled in the heart of the city, was the scene of intense preparations. The young and determined agents were busy laying the foundation of an organization that would shape Israel's future. I was one of them, a young man whose heart beat in tune with the aspirations of our people.

«Do you feel the tension in the air?» Yitzhak, a longtime colleague, asked as we pored over the detailed plans of upcoming operations.

«Yes,» I replied, staring at the maps scattered on the table. «Every move we make could change the course of history.»

The dim light of the meeting room cast dancing shadows on the concentrated faces of the agents. The discussions were lively, swinging between defensive and offensive strategies. The creation of the State of Israel had been proclaimed with fervor, but the reality on the ground imposed immense challenges. Regional tensions, imminent threats, and the absolute necessity to secure our existence pressed us from every side. I recalled the long nights spent studying the military patterns of neighboring countries, analyzing every detail to anticipate their moves. The mission to protect our nation came with an overwhelming responsibility, but also with unshakable determination. Every Mossad agent was aware of the importance of their role in this quest.

«We must be ready for anything,» Yitzhak declared, breaking the heavy silence in the room. «The survival of our people depends on it.»

His words resonated deeply within me. I had joined the Mossad with a clear idea of contributing to the security of our nation, but reality far exceeded my initial expectations. The first days were a total immersion into a world of secrets, strategies, and personal sacrifices. The bonds between agents were forged through shared experiences, creating an indispensable brotherhood in the face of external threats. The cool night breeze drifted through the slightly open windows, carrying with it the distant sounds of war preparations. Soldiers patrolled the streets, and the outskirts of Tel Aviv were transformed into highly secured zones. Every movement was monitored, every conversation scrutinized. The distrust of the enemy was palpable, but it also fueled our determination to remain vigilant and ready to act.

«Have you heard the latest news from Jerusalem?» Yitzhak suddenly asked, changing the subject.

I nodded, my mind already on high alert. Jerusalem, with its strategic and symbolic importance, was at the heart of the new state's concerns. Tensions there were heightened, and every advance or retreat on the ground had direct repercussions on our collective morale.

«Preparations are underway to strengthen defenses,» I replied. «We cannot afford to be caught off guard.»

We continued discussing various strategies, each idea being scrutinized and analyzed meticulously. The creation of Mossad was a direct response to the challenges before us. We were not just intelligence agents, but the guardians of our nation's survival. Every operation, every mission, was an essential piece of the complex puzzle of national security. Hours passed, but the energy in the room did not wane. The discussions were punctuated by moments of contemplative silence, where each of us reflected on the significance of our future actions. The anticipation of what was to come weighed heavily, but it was balanced by an unwavering faith in our mission.

As dawn broke on the horizon, tinting the sky with shades of pink, I felt a deep gratitude to those who had worked to make this moment possible. The birth of a nation was not just a political event but the culmination of years of struggle, sacrifice, and resilience. As a young Mossad agent, I was proud to be part of this history, aware that each day would bring new challenges, but also new opportunities to contribute to the security and prosperity of our nascent Israel.

«Top Secret» Operations from 1948 to Today

The Secret History of Mossad

Chapter II

First Missions

The first light of dawn slipped through the shutters of our office, gently illuminating the focused faces around the meeting table. Tel Aviv, still asleep, was starting to wake up, but inside Mossad, the agitation was already palpable. I sat across from David, our deputy director, whose piercing gaze seemed to scrutinize every detail of our discussion.

«We have received new directives,» he began in a calm but firm voice. «Our first missions must establish our presence and demonstrate our effectiveness.»

I felt my heart beat faster. This was the long-awaited moment, my first steps into the field. The previous weeks had been filled with rigorous training and psychological tests, but nothing had prepared me for this exact moment. The atmosphere was heavy with responsibility, each word exchanged carrying the weight of our national mission.

«What are our immediate priorities?» asked a masculine voice next to me. It was Amir, a colleague whose determination matched his efficiency.

«The priority is to infiltrate enemy networks,» David replied, flipping through the files in front of him. «We need to obtain crucial information about military movements and the intentions of neighboring nations.»

The office was silent for a moment, each of us absorbing the magnitude of the tasks ahead. I still recalled the long nights spent studying strategic maps and analyzing intelligence reports. Every detail mattered; every piece of information could make the difference between victory and defeat.

«Our first mission is in Jerusalem,» David continued. «We have intelligence on a double agent operating undercover. It is essential to uncover his true intentions and neutralize any potential threat.»

I looked up, meeting David's determined gaze. This was a unique opportunity to prove my worth, to truly contribute to the security of our nation. Excitement and apprehension swirled within me, creating a palpable tension.

«I'm ready,» I finally said, my voice betraying a hint of emotion. «Trust me, I won't let you down.»

Amir nodded, and a slight smile appeared on his face. «We believe in you,» he said. «Welcome to the team.»

The days that followed were a whirlwind of preparations. The field operations were planned with military precision, each step carefully orchestrated to minimize risks and maximize results. Practical training sessions multiplied, simulating real-life scenarios where speed and discretion were paramount. I remember one particularly intense session where we had to infiltrate a suspect warehouse, simulate a capture, and extract vital information while undercover. David's relentless coaching, Amir's precise feedback, all contributed to honing our skills. Each agent developed a particular expertise, whether in cryptology, survival, or counterintelligence. One evening, as I was heading home, I couldn't help but reflect on the gravity of our missions. The streetlights cast long shadows on the deserted sidewalks, and the heavy silence of the city deepened my thoughts. The fate of our nation now rested in our hands, and every decision, every action counted.

«You seem thoughtful,» Amir suddenly remarked, appearing at my side as if by magic.

«Yes, I'm thinking about our mission in Jerusalem,» I replied, trying to hide my anxiety. «It's an immense responsibility.»

«True,» he agreed. «But remember why we're doing this. To protect our people, to ensure the survival of our nation.»

His words resonated within me, somewhat easing my worries. The mission in Jerusalem was not just a task; it was a sacred duty. The challenges were immense, but the hope and determination of our team were our greatest strength. Weeks passed, and the excitement grew as the date of the mission approached. Final checks were carried out, and the plans were finely adjusted to guarantee success. David held one last meeting before our departure, bringing together all the agents involved.

«We leave at sunrise tomorrow,» he announced, his gaze sweeping over each attentive face. «Remember, discretion is our most valuable ally. Our actions must remain invisible to the enemy, but their impact will be significant.»

The day arrived, and I felt a mix of excitement and nervousness. I put on my uniform, the Mossad badge gleaming under the harsh light of the briefing room. The agents prepared, exchanging determined looks and silent encouragements.

«Good luck,» Amir whispered as he passed by me.

«You too,» I replied, lightly shaking his hand.

We boarded the plane that would take us to Jerusalem, the takeoff marking the beginning of our first real mission. Through the window, the city stretched as far as the eye could see, its lights twinkling like earthly stars. My mind was a whirlwind of thoughts, but one idea guided my actions: success. The flight went smoothly, and soon we landed discreetly at Tel Aviv airport. Each step towards our destination was filled with tension, but also with unwavering determination. The mission in Jerusalem was more than just an operation; it was an act of faith in our new nation. Upon our arrival, the warmth of the climate and the bustle of the city contrasted with the methodical calm of our preparation. The cobbled streets of Jerusalem were lively, and every corner seemed to hold secrets. We blended into the crowd, measuring every move, every suspicious glance.

«Remember our objectives,» David whispered in my ear, his warm breath against my neck. «Find the double agent, gather information, and return safely.»

I nodded, ready to dive into the unknown. The first days of our mission were a delicate dance between infiltration and observation, each minute a struggle to remain imperceptible. The narrow streets and crowded markets offered perfect hiding spots but also constant challenges to maintain our cover. One evening, as we discreetly observed a suspicious meeting in a quiet café, I caught a glimmer of hope. The double agent appeared, exchanging information with an unidentified individual. My heart raced, but I remembered Amir's words: «Stay focused, keep a cool head.»

«We've got what we need,» David murmured, his eyes fixed on the scene. «Prepare for the next step.»

The capture of the double agent was swift and efficient, thanks to flawless coordination and meticulous preparation. The information we gathered revealed crucial details about the military intentions of neighboring nations, strengthening our strategic position. Returning to Tel Aviv with the obtained data was a moment of quiet triumph. The satisfaction of contributing to our nation's security was immense, but I knew this was only the beginning. Each successful mission strengthened our determination, but the challenges remained immense and inevitable. As I walked through the bustling streets of Tel Aviv upon my return, I felt a pride mixed with deep gratitude for my colleagues and those who had worked for the creation of our state. The past and present sacrifices were reflected in every smile, every handshake exchanged within Mossad. The first missions had laid the foundation for what we would become, a team united by a common goal and an unshakable faith in our mission. Tel Aviv, with its unique blend of modernity and tradition, remained the beating heart of our organization, a symbol of resilience and determination in the face of future uncertainties.

«Top Secret» Operations from 1948 to Today

The Secret History of Mossad

Chapter III

The Hunt for Eichmann

The winter of 1960 envelops Buenos Aires in a biting cold. The city's streets vibrate with incessant activity, concealing beneath their bustle the secrets we are seeking to uncover. Like a complex puzzle, every dark corner, every lively café, could hold an essential piece of our quest. I sit in a modest office, surrounded by detailed maps and confidential files, the weight of the mission pressing on my shoulders.

«We must locate Eichmann quickly,» declares David, the deputy director of Mossad, his voice resonating with quiet authority. «Every day counts.»

I nod, feeling the palpable tension in the air. The hunt for Adolf Eichmann, the logistical mastermind behind the Final Solution, is much more than a simple operation. It is a historic mission, an act of justice for millions of lost lives. The preparations are meticulous, every detail scrutinized with almost surgical precision.

«Intelligence indicates that he is hiding under the identity of Ricardo Clement,» David continues, pointing to a blurry photograph on the wall. «Foreman at an auto factory in San Fernando.»

Amir, our cryptology specialist, interrupts the meeting with a succinct but crucial report. His eyes gleam with unshakable determination as he presents the latest analyses of intercepted communications.

«We have decrypted several coded messages that strengthen our belief that Eichmann is indeed here,» he explains. «He is using sophisticated codes, but we have cracked their meaning.»

Hours turn into days, and nights into sleepless vigilance. Mossad agents discreetly infiltrate the social and professional circles of Argentina, weaving a network of informants and reliable contacts. Every meeting, every exchange, is a piece of the puzzle that brings us closer to our target. One evening, as the rain drums against the windows of our temporary office, Yitzhak, a seasoned agent, returns with encouraging news.

«We have a solid lead,» he announces, wiping his wet coat. «An anonymous source has provided the exact address of his residence.»

My heart races. After so many weeks of hard work, we finally have a precise location. The mission that follows is risky but essential. We must capture Eichmann without alerting the Argentine authorities to avoid a major diplomatic crisis. The preparations for the operation are intense. We draft a detailed plan, every step scrutinized to minimize risks. The coordination between teams is crucial, each move synchronized to perfection. The days leading up to the operation are marked by growing tension, a silent anticipation of what might happen.

«We leave at dawn,» David declares during our last meeting before the operation. «Discretion is our top priority. Once captured, we must bring him back to Israel without leaving a trace.»

The morning arrives, the air fresh and filled with promise. We approach Ricardo Clement's residence with military precision. The streets are quiet, almost deserted, offering perfect cover for our infiltration. I take a deep breath, my thoughts focused on the mission ahead.

«Team, move in,» orders David, his gaze fixed on the front door.

We enter the house with absolute discretion, our movements fluid and silent. Every step is calculated, every action controlled. Inside, all is calm, an almost familiar atmosphere that belies the gravity of the moment. Suddenly, a door creaks open, and there, standing before us, is Eichmann.

«Farewell,» he murmurs, a glimmer of recognition in his eyes. «You have finally succeeded.»

Without wasting a second, we spring into action. The exchange is brief but intense, a silent struggle between two opposing forces. Eichmann tries to resist, but our preparation and determination prevail. He is captured, our mission accomplished. Returning to Israel is an equally delicate operation. We must ensure that our capture remains secret, avoiding any alert that could compromise our cover. Every kilometer traveled is a silent victory, a step toward long-awaited justice. Upon our arrival, the atmosphere at Mossad is electrifying. Agents celebrate quietly, aware of the importance of this success for national security and collective memory. Eichmann will be tried in Jerusalem, a symbolic act of justice for generations of victims.

For me, this operation marks a turning point in my career. The hunt for Eichmann not only allowed me to prove my worth within Mossad, but it also strengthened my resolve to protect our nation from all threats. Every successful mission brings us closer to our ultimate goal: ensuring the survival and prosperity of the State of Israel. The months that follow are imbued with a sense of pride and increased responsibility. Eichmann's capture has bolstered Mossad's reputation, not only in Israel but also on the international stage. This success has solidified our position as one of the most effective and feared intelligence services in the world. However, this victory is not without consequences. The challenges are just beginning, and every success opens the door to new threats and new missions. But the hunt for Eichmann remains etched in my memory as the first great test of our organization, a test we passed brilliantly thanks to our dedication and expertise. As I reflect on the events of the past, I realize how much this operation has shaped our identity as Mossad agents. We are not just spies but the guardians of a young and vulnerable nation, determined to survive and prosper despite the obstacles imposed by history and persistent enemies.

The Secret History of Mossad

Chapter IV

The MiG 21 Coup

Winter 1965, Buenos Aires, unfolds under a leaden sky, each raindrop seeming to weigh heavier on the shoulders of those working in the shadows. The bustling streets barely conceal the internal agitation of Mossad, where every detail matters, and mistakes are not an option. The operation to seize a formidable Iraqi MiG 21 is in motion, and the palpable mix of excitement and tension fills the air. Seated around the conference table, faces reflect both determination and caution. David, our deputy director, draws precise lines on a map annotated with cryptic symbols. His measured movements reveal unshakable confidence, a reflection of the mission's complexity.

«We cannot allow Iraq to strengthen its military arsenal,» he declares in a calm yet authoritative voice. «This MiG 21 could upset the regional balance. We must act with the precision of a Swiss watch.»

The words resonate like an echo in the room, each of us feeling the weight of responsibility. Recruiting

27

the pilot is our first crucial step. Amir, our recruitment specialist, presents a shortlist of potential candidates, each name scrutinized with an almost obsessive focus. After hours of intense deliberation, one name emerges: Captain Mounir Redfa. An Iraqi pilot whose ambitions, frustrated by his Christian faith, make him vulnerable to Mossad's propositions. The process of recruiting Mounir is a chess game, each move calculated to win his trust without arousing suspicion. Discreet meetings in quiet cafés, carefully encrypted email exchanges, and seemingly casual discussions on mundane topics form our cover. Every interaction is a delicate dance between manipulation and sincerity, each gesture calculated to weave an unbreakable web of trust. One evening, as the moon faintly illuminates the deserted streets of Buenos Aires, I find myself sitting across from Mounir in a small, secluded restaurant. His eyes betray a mix of suspicion and hope.

«I understand your situation,» Amir begins, breaking the ice with controlled confidence. «We can offer you a new identity, a life without fear or constraints.»

Mounir listens intently, his gaze oscillating between determination and vulnerability.

«But what about my family?» he asks, his voice betraying a hint of anxiety. «If I betray them, they will be in danger.»

The words hang in the heavy air, and the room seems to close in on us. David intervenes with a reassuring proposal, his words weaving a safety net around our request.

«We guarantee your family's safety,» he affirms. «In exchange, you fly the MiG 21 for us. This is a unique opportunity to contribute to the security of our nation while ensuring the well-being of your loved ones.»

After long hours of silent negotiations, Mounir finally nods. The mission is launched, and every detail is orchestrated with military precision. Logistical preparations are conducted with ruthless efficiency: a private plane is chartered, forged documents are prepared, and a perfectly charted route is planned to avoid detection. Every step is one closer to realizing our objective, every second a race against the clock. On the appointed day, dawn rises over Tel Aviv with a silent promise of success. Mounir is escorted to the plane disguised as flight crew, his calm and assured movements betraying a newfound confidence. The passing glances of onlookers are curious but indifferent, a veil of normalcy covering our daring operation.

«Good flight, Mounir,» Amir murmurs as he approaches him. «Don't look back. Everything is going as planned.»

The plane takes off without incident, carrying with it our hope and determination. The ascent is a poignant metaphor for our mission: climbing the peaks of caution and strategy to achieve our goal without leaving a trace. Communications are discreet, every message exchanged is one step closer to the capture of the much-coveted MiG 21. The execution of the operation is a silent ballet of coordinated movements. Mossad agents, hidden in the shadows, watch every detail with razor-sharp acuity. Mounir, aware of his mission, flies the plane with remarkable precision, unaware of the full ramifications of his actions. The capture of the MiG 21 unfolds with near-perfect fluidity, every step carried out with disconcerting efficiency.

Upon our return to Israel, the reception is quiet but filled with relief. The MiG 21, the emblem of our success, is quickly integrated into our arsenal, strengthening our strategic position in the region. The mission is hailed as a tactical feat, solidifying Mossad's reputation as a ruthless and ingenious intelligence service. International reactions are mixed, ranging from tacit admiration to veiled suspicion, but our absolute discretion maintains the secrecy of our operation. For me, this mission represents a decisive turning point. The hunt and capture of the MiG 21 demonstrate not only our ability to execute complex operations but also our unwavering determination to protect our nation from any threat. Every agent involved in this operation feels a quiet pride, a recognition of the crucial role we play in the survival and prosperity of the State of Israel.

However, this success is not without its share of challenges and personal reflections. The responsibility of possessing a warplane in enemy territory weighs heavily, and the need to remain vigilant in the face of potential reprisals pushes us to constantly sharpen our skills and innovate our methods. Mossad, now strengthened by this victory, continues to evolve, adapting its strategies to anticipate and neutralize emerging threats.

As I gaze out over the vast horizons of Tel Aviv from my office, I realize how this operation has not only strengthened our arsenal but also cemented our role as guardians of a young and vulnerable nation. Mossad, with its ingenuity and determination, has established itself as a formidable force, ready to do whatever it takes to ensure Israel's security and longevity. And I, as an agent of this organization, am determined to continue this mission with the same zeal and vigilance, knowing that each success brings us closer to our ultimate goal: the survival and prosperity of our state.

The Secret History of Mossad

Chapter V

Spies in Enemy Territory

Dusk slowly spreads over Damascus, enveloping the city in a mysterious twilight. It is here that our new mission begins, a dive into the heart of hostile territory where every step could be fatal. The narrow, winding streets of the old city offer a maze of secrets and dangers, a real puzzle for anyone daring to venture there without proper preparation. As a Mossad agent, my role is to navigate this perilous environment with absolute discretion, like a chameleon adapting to its surroundings. The first days of our deployment are a delicate dance between vigilance and infiltration. Every encounter, every exchange, is a piece of the puzzle we must assemble to achieve our objective without raising suspicion. I particularly remember the evening when, disguised as a foreign businessman, I found myself face to face with a key figure in the enemy network. The tension was palpable, each word as sharp as a sword strike in the silence of the night.

"You're looking for specific information, aren't you?" he asked, fixing his gaze intensely on mine, his voice betraying a mix of curiosity and suspicion.

"Yes," I replied calmly, keeping my cool despite the chill running down my spine. "I'm looking for reliable contacts in this region. Someone who can help me better understand the local dynamics."

The conversation flowed with feigned ease, each phrase carefully crafted to avoid revealing my true intentions. The streets of Damascus became the stage for our shadow play, where every gesture and glance could mean the difference between success and failure. The subterfuge used to remain unnoticed multiplied, turning our daily life into a series of meticulously orchestrated masks and disguises. One morning, as the sun timidly broke on the horizon, I came face to face with a stark reality: dangers were omnipresent, and the risks, very real. A failed mission could not only compromise our operation but also put my life and that of my colleagues in jeopardy. The loneliness of the spy in enemy territory weighed heavily on my shoulders, every decision made in the shadows reinforcing the sense of isolation.

"Sometimes I wonder if it's all worth it," Amir murmured during one of our rare private conversations. "The loneliness is unbearable, and doubt creeps in."

I looked at him, fully understanding his feelings. The mission in enemy territory was a constant battle against the shadows of uncertainty and fear. But the determination to protect our nation and honor past sacrifices pushed us forward, despite the trials. Nights in Damascus were a blend of adrenaline and deep reflection. Every mission accomplished was a silent victory, but every potential failure was a painful lesson. I remember one particular mission where we had to infiltrate a group of local resistance fighters to gather vital information. The risks were high, and the slightest mistake could cost us dearly. Unexpected encounters with members of the enemy network added another layer of complexity to our already arduous task.

"We must stay focused and leave no room for error," insisted David during our daily briefings. "Every piece of information brings us closer to our goal, but also closer to danger."

The loneliness of the spy is not only physical but psychological as well. Moments of doubt follow one another, questioning the validity of our methods and the morality of our actions. Yet the deep conviction that we are doing what is necessary for the survival of our nation keeps us on a straight path, even when the night's shadows seem ready to engulf us. One evening, as I discreetly observed a clandestine meeting in a quiet café, a flash of information upended our careful planning. An internal source had leaked crucial details about enemy movements, offering a unique opportunity to strike where it hurt most. The tension ratcheted up, every second counting in this race against time.

"This is our chance," Amir whispered as he passed by me. "We must act quickly before the opportunity slips away."

The preparation for this attack was a race against the clock, every step carried out with surgical precision. The plans were refined, resources allocated with ruthless efficiency, and coordination between teams was flawless. The success of this operation could change the game, strengthening our strategic position in the region and significantly weakening the enemy's capabilities. On the day of the operation, the air was charged with electric energy. The streets of Damascus were eerily calm, as if the city was holding its breath before the storm. We moved discreetly, our movements fluid and silent, ready to strike at the precise moment when the enemy was most vulnerable. The adrenaline surged, every fiber of my being on high alert.

"It's now or never," David murmured as we neared our target. "Stay focused and leave no trace."

The attack was swift and efficient, a silent blow that struck directly at the heart of enemy operations. The reactions were immediate, a strategic confusion that disoriented our adversaries and bolstered our superiority. The success of this mission was a quiet victory, a demonstration of our efficiency and determination to protect our nation at all costs. International reactions were not long in coming. Our allies praised our audacity and ingenuity, while our adversaries wondered how we had managed to strike with such precision. Mossad's reputation as a ruthless and ingenious intelligence service was further cemented, and we became a respected and feared shadow on the world stage.

For me, this mission was a source of immense pride but also an awareness of the challenges ahead. Infiltrating enemy territory, the constant dangers, and the subterfuge required to remain unnoticed shaped our identity as Mossad agents. Every completed operation was another stone added to the edifice of our legend, but it was also a brutal reminder of the personal sacrifices and inherent risks of our profession. As I gazed upon the bustling streets of Tel Aviv upon my return, I felt a mix of excitement and deep reflection. The loneliness of the spy in enemy territory had left an indelible mark on my soul, constantly reminding me why we do what we do. Mossad, with its global network of infiltrated agents, continues to evolve and adapt, ready to face new threats and ensure our nation's security at all costs.

The Secret History of Mossad

Chapter VI

The Six-Day War

The sky over Tel Aviv is tinged with an incandescent orange as the dawn of June 1967 rises over a region in turmoil. The air is thick with palpable tension, a silent electricity buzzing beneath the city's calm surface. The streets, usually bustling, seem to hold their breath, as if the entire city is awaiting the imminent gunshot. It is in this atmosphere of uncertainty that our Mossad team prepares to play a crucial role in what will become one of the most resounding victories in our history. Sitting in the Mossad briefing room, my heart races. David, our deputy director, unfurls a series of maps and strategic reports before us. Every line drawn, every mark on these maps represents a meticulously planned step to ensure Israeli supremacy in record time.

«This is the decisive moment,» he announces, his voice slicing through the silence of the room with an intensity that grabs everyone's attention. «Our intelligence has identified the weaknesses in Egyptian defenses. We must strike where it hurts before they can react.»

I glance around, seeing the faces of my colleagues, reflecting both determination and apprehension. The preparations have been kept secret, every move orchestrated with military precision. Months of gathering information, discreet infiltrations, and painstaking analysis converge at this critical moment. The adrenaline builds within me as I grasp the importance of our mission.

«We have a 48-hour window of opportunity,» explains Amir, our cryptology specialist. «Intercepted transmissions indicate a massive concentration of enemy forces in the Sinai. If we act now, we can disrupt their lines and gain a decisive strategic advantage.»

Amir's words hit the mark, igniting the fire of our resolve. We know every second counts, and the slightest hesitation could be costly. War is looming fast, and our role is more pivotal than ever. The preparations follow one another at a rapid pace. Teams are deployed to airports to secure airbases, information is relayed in real time, and every Mossad agent is on high alert. The nights become sleepless, punctuated by tactical discussions and relentless rechecking of attack plans. The unity and cohesion of our team are tested, but they remain unshakable. One morning, as the sun begins to rise over the horizon, the alarm sounds in our command center. Israeli planes are ready, their engines humming like impatient predators. The tension reaches its peak, each heartbeat seeming to reverberate through the briefing room.

«It's time,» orders David, his determined gaze fixed on the control screens. «We will strike before the enemy can retaliate.»

The pilots take their positions, and commands are given with surgical precision. The planes take off in a perfectly synchronized ballet, soaring into the morning sky like golden arrows aimed at their targets. The rumble of the engines and the palpable excitement fill the air, as each agent feels a surge of adrenaline that transcends fear. Through the windows, the city of Tel Aviv quickly fades away, replaced by the desert landscapes of the Sinai. The coordinates are clear, the targets identified with deadly accuracy. The role of intelligence proves crucial, as our precise information allows for a lightning strike that catches the enemy off guard.

«The defenses are in disarray,» Amir shouts from the command center, his eyes glued to the screens showing the enemy's disorganization. «We've gained the advantage.»

The scene before my eyes is both magnificent and terrifying. Israeli planes appear on the horizon, striking with speed and overwhelming efficiency. Explosions light up the sky, and within a few hours, Israel's air superiority is sealed. The enemy radars are in chaos, their air defenses obliterated in a flash, leaving their military infrastructure in ruins. Emotions within our team are mixed. Joy and pride blend with exhaustion and relief. We have accomplished what seemed impossible, thanks to months of hard work and unwavering dedication. Animated discussions begin, with everyone sharing their thoughts and reflections on the operation's success.

«It's incredible,» exclaims Yitzhak, a seasoned agent. «We really made a difference. Our work paid off, and our nation is safe, at least for now.»

I nod, feeling a deep sense of satisfaction. Yet deep down, a lingering worry remains. The Six-Day War is just one chapter in our history, and every victory comes with new threats and challenges. Mossad's role in this swift victory has been crucial, but it's clear our mission is far from over. The international fallout is immediate. Our allies praise our efficiency and resolve, while our adversaries are forced to rethink their strategies. Mossad's reputation as a ruthless and ingenious intelligence service is cemented, and we are now seen as a formidable force on the world stage.

For me, this war marks a personal turning point. Every successful mission strengthens my determination to protect our nation, but it also leaves an indelible mark on my mind. The memories of secret preparations, sleepless nights, and critical decisions remain etched in me, shaping my career and worldview.

As I reflect on the results of our work from my office, I realize the magnitude of what we have accomplished. The Six-Day War has proven that our dedication and expertise can alter the course of history. But it has also reminded me of the fragility of peace and the need to remain ever vigilant against the threats that loom over our nation. The months that follow are marked by the consolidation of our gains and constant preparation for future operations. Mossad, now bolstered by this resounding victory, continues to evolve and adapt, ready to face upcoming challenges with the same determination and verbal agility that allowed us to triumph in this lightning war. The Six-Day War remains an iconic period in our history, a shining example of the power of intelligence and the unyielding will to protect our nation.

As a Mossad agent, I am proud to have played a part in this victory, knowing that every mission completed adds another stone to the edifice of our secret legend. And as the days go by, I know that our mission continues, fueled by the same determination and passion that led us to triumph in this historic war.

The Secret History of Mossad

Chapter VII

Munich: The Shock

The winter of 1972 strikes Munich with relentless cold, wrapping the city in a shroud of sadness and palpable tension. The Olympic Games, once a symbol of peace and global unity, have turned into a silent nightmare, marking a dark turning point in the history of our nation. I sit in the somber Mossad office, my thoughts swirling like the snowflakes accumulating outside. The announcement of the terrorist attack still echoes in my ears, a haunting reminder of violence and despair.

"This is a hard blow for all of us," murmurs Yitzhak, my longtime colleague, breaking the heavy silence in the room. His sorrowful eyes meet mine, reflecting a shared pain that words struggle to express.

I nod, my heart heavy. The attack at the Munich Olympics was not only an assault on Israeli athletes but a direct attack on our very existence. The nine hostages, taken in a live televised horror, were more than victims; they symbolized our fragility and vulnerability in the face of enemies determined to spread terror and chaos. The Mossad's preparations following this event unfold in a somber atmosphere, every decision made under the shadow of pain and anger. Internal discussions are filled with fierce determination to never again find ourselves powerless against terrorism. The walls of our office seem to absorb our frustration, every conversation an attempt to channel our rage into concrete, effective actions.

"We must intensify our efforts to track down and eliminate those who hide in the shadows," declares David, our deputy director, his voice grave and resolute. "The Munich attack has exposed our weaknesses. It's time to strengthen our methods and show our enemies that we will never stand idly by."

The impact of Munich on me and Mossad is deep and enduring. Every agent feels a renewed urgency, a flame of determination that burns more intensely after this tragedy. The feelings of helplessness and anger transform into an implacable thirst for justice, a drive to never allow such horror to occur again. I remember the sleepless nights spent analyzing every detail of the attack, searching for clues, for gaps in the defenses that could have been exploited to prevent this catastrophe. Emotions ran high, with every discovery offering a glimmer of hope in the darkness of our despair. Conversations with my colleagues are now tinged with a new intensity, each exchange aimed at refining our strategies and reinforcing our cohesion in the face of adversity.

"We need to adopt a more proactive approach," insists Amir during a late-night meeting, his determined gaze fixed on the strategic map laid out before him. "We can't just react to attacks—we must anticipate them. Let's use our intelligence to predict enemy movements before they materialize."

His words resonate deeply within me, awakening a new perspective on our mission. The Munich attack is not just a tragic event but a catalyst pushing us to evolve, rethink our methods, and strengthen our resilience. Internal discussions multiply, each person bringing their expertise to build a more robust defense and a more targeted offense. The following weeks are marked by an intensification of our efforts. Agents are deployed to neighboring countries with increased discretion, each infiltration a piece of the complex puzzle of our new anti-terrorism strategy. Constant dangers and the subterfuge used to remain unnoticed become our daily routine, a delicate dance between survival and operational efficiency.

One evening, while discreetly monitoring a suspicious gathering in a Berlin café, we receive an internal alert. A terrorist cell is about to carry out an attack similar to Munich. My heart tightens at the thought of reliving that nightmare, but determination overtakes fear. I remember the faces of the hostages, the tears, the terror, and I know I cannot stand idle.

"We must act immediately," orders David, his gaze fixed on the surveillance screens. "Prepare for an infiltration and neutralization operation."

The tension rises as we plan the operation with surgical precision. Every detail is scrutinized, every risk meticulously evaluated. Adrenaline surges through my veins as I prepare to plunge once more into the shadows, determined to prevent another tragedy. The emotions are a mix of fear and courage, a constant duality that defines our existence as Mossad agents. The execution of the operation is a perfectly orchestrated ballet, every movement the result of months of preparation and dedication. Real-time discussions with my colleagues are charged with a newfound intensity, as every second counts in this race against time to save innocent lives. The scene unfolds with an almost hypnotic fluidity, the stakes higher than ever.

At the end of the mission, a wave of relief and satisfaction washes over us. We successfully neutralized the terrorist cell before they could recreate the horror of Munich. The emotions are intense, oscillating between the joy of having fulfilled our duty and the sadness of the lives lost, even those of our enemies. The reactions in Israel are immediate, a surge of gratitude and recognition for Mossad, but also a renewed awareness of the dangers that lie ahead. For me, Munich represents a major turning point in my career and in Mossad's history. The personal impact is immense, strengthening my determination to protect our nation while confronting the brutal realities of war and terrorism. Every mission completed builds our secret legend, one made of sacrifice, courage, and an unyielding will to survive and prosper.

As I reflect on the events, I realize how much Munich has transformed our organization. Mossad has gone from being a discreet intelligence service to a formidable force, ready to do whatever it takes to ensure the security of our nation. The memories of sleepless nights, intense discussions, and dangerous missions remain etched in my mind, constantly reminding me why we do what we do. As the days pass and peace temporarily returns to our land, I know the challenges are just beginning. Munich marked a new chapter in our history, a chapter where intelligence and action combined to create an unyielding defense against all threats. As a Mossad agent, I am proud to be part of this legend, knowing that every mission completed brings us closer to our ultimate goal: the survival and prosperity of the State of Israel.

The Secret History of Mossad

Chapter VIII

The Vengeance Begins

The twilight of my existence within Mossad is now shadowed by something darker than ever before. The year 1972 has given way to a decision that will forever alter the course of our history. The tragedy of Munich, etched into our memories like a deep wound, has awakened within us an insatiable thirst for justice. This marked the beginning of an era where vengeance became our driving force, where every action was guided by the resolve never to endure such a tragedy again.

Sitting around the conference table, the silence is heavy, thick with palpable tension. David, our deputy director, speaks with a firm voice, slicing through the silence like a knife through butter. "We can no longer remain passive in the face of such barbarity," he declares, his determination unshakable. "It's time to strike back, to show our enemies that we will never stand idly by."

The preparations for these elimination operations are meticulous, with every detail scrutinized with military precision. Meetings follow one another, strategies are drawn up, and each agent is tasked with a specific mission. The decision to launch these operations is born from a mixture of anger and resilience, a double-edged sword that pushes us forward despite the moral dilemmas that assail us.

"We must be certain of our targets," Amir, our intelligence specialist, emphasizes. "The slightest mistake could cost innocent lives and jeopardize our mission."

I feel the weight of his words on my shoulders, a tremendous responsibility that drives me to exceed my own limits. Moral dilemmas are ever-present, as every elimination mission is an internal struggle between justice and revenge. Yet, the collective determination propels us forward, ensuring that we don't let anger blind us but instead use it as a force to protect our nation.

The first missions are orchestrated with ruthless efficiency. Each operation unfolds like a symphony of coordination and precision, with every agent playing their part with impressive mastery. The action scenes are swift, enemies neutralized before they even realize what's happening. The adrenaline runs high, with every successful mission reinforcing our determination to continue this quest for justice.

One evening, as I return to my apartment after a successful operation, I find myself staring into a mirror, contemplating the reflection of a changed man. The lines on my face bear the marks of fatigue, but my eyes shine with renewed determination. «Is this really justice, or is it just revenge?» I murmur to myself, the question swirling in my mind like a silent storm.

Noticing my turmoil, Amir joins me and places a comforting hand on my shoulder. "The line between justice and revenge is thin," he says softly. "But as long as we are protecting our people, every action matters."

The following nights are marked by an intensification of our operations. Mossad agents are deployed to neighboring countries with increased discretion and efficiency, each mission another piece in the complex puzzle of our anti-terrorism strategy. Subterfuge becomes our daily existence, a delicate dance between shadow and light, where every move is calculated to go unnoticed while achieving our objectives.

During a particularly perilous mission in Syria, we had to infiltrate a paramilitary group known for its close ties to terrorist organizations. The tension was palpable, with every gesture potentially a matter of life or death. The constant dangers and high risks only strengthened our resilience but also deepened our isolation. Far from our loved ones and the safety of Tel Aviv, we were the silent shadows working in darkness to protect our nation.

"Stay sharp," David murmured during a nighttime elimination operation, his voice betraying a rare nervousness. "Any mistake could cost us dearly."

The success of the mission was a quiet triumph, a victory etched in the shadows of the night. But it also left an indelible mark on our minds, a trace of pain and guilt mingled with the satisfaction of having done our duty. Personal reflections on justice and vengeance grew more frequent, as each agent faced their own moral dilemmas, seeking a balance between duty and humanity.

One day, as I walked past the Munich memorial, the memories of that tragedy returned to haunt me with searing intensity. The names of the hostages engraved on the stones, their faces frozen in eternal pain, were a brutal reminder of what we were fighting for. Vengeance cannot bring back the innocent, but it can prevent other similar tragedies from occurring.

"We do what we must," David affirmed during a post-mission meeting, his determined gaze fixed on the tired faces of his agents. "For every life lost, we do everything in our power to protect our people."

As the months passed, each successful mission reinforced our reputation and efficiency. Mossad became a formidable shadow, an invisible yet omnipresent force capable of striking with surgical precision where it mattered most. Reactions in Israel were mixed, a combination of gratitude and fear, recognition and questioning. Internal discussions within Mossad were intense, with every agent grappling to understand and justify the necessary sacrifices to ensure our nation's security.

For me, this period was a test of inner strength. The line between justice and vengeance blurred more and more with each mission completed, feeding both my determination and my moral questions. Personal reflections on the meaning of our actions and the nature of justice accompanied me day and night, pushing me to seek a fragile balance between duty and humanity.

As I gaze out over the bustling streets of Tel Aviv from my office, a sense of pride mixed with deep melancholy washes over me. The vengeance we started has become an unrelenting pursuit, a mission to protect our nation at all costs. Personal sacrifices and moral dilemmas have become an integral part of our existence as Mossad agents, shaping our identity and strengthening our resolve to never again let our nation become vulnerable.

Each mission completed adds another stone to the edifice of our secret legend, a legend built on courage, resilience, and an unyielding will to protect our people. The vengeance that began in response to the horror of Munich has become a driving force, a silent determination that pushes us forward despite the obstacles and sacrifices. And as the days go by, I know that our mission continues, fueled by the same intensity and determination that led us into this silent war for the survival and prosperity of the State of Israel.

The Secret History of Mossad

Chapter IX

The Lillehammer Affair

The winter of 1973 blankets Lillehammer in a frozen silence, snowflakes dancing through the still air. This picturesque Norwegian town, known for its idyllic landscapes and harsh winters, becomes the stage for a clandestine operation that will forever mark Mossad's history and my own path. The atmosphere is heavy, charged with tension that contrasts sharply with the apparent tranquility of the snow-covered streets. Seated in a dimly lit meeting room, I stare intently at the plans laid out before me. Every detail has been analyzed with obsessive precision, each step meticulously planned to avoid fatal mistakes. The Lillehammer operation, meant to be a mission of precision, spirals into an irreversible tragedy that leaves deep scars within our organization and on my soul.

"We must act quickly and discreetly," declares David, our deputy director, his voice as sharp as the winter wind outside. "Salameh is a direct threat to our national security. His capture is imperative."

David's words thunder through the room, triggering a cascade of internal reflections. The hunt for Ali Hassan Salameh, a key figure in the PLO and mastermind of the Munich attacks, has become our top priority. The preparations are intense, with every agent mobilized by an unshakable determination. The risks are immense, but the urgency of the mission pushes us beyond our usual limits. In the weeks leading up to the operation, we hold secret meetings, conduct covert infiltrations, and gather intelligence. We pinpoint Salameh's location in Beirut, amidst the war-torn landscape of Syria. Roadblocks manned by various militias make infiltration nearly impossible. Still, we push forward, determined to overcome every obstacle with unwavering ingenuity.

One foggy February morning, the team is finally ready. Six agents, including myself, are dispatched to Lillehammer, disguised as foreign technicians, ready to execute a mission that could seal our fate. The logistical preparations are meticulous, with every detail reviewed to avoid failure. The silent exchange of glances between team members reveals a shared anxiety, a collective awareness of the stakes and the dangers ahead.

"Remember," David murmurs, his determined gaze fixed on the snow-covered landscape, "the slightest mistake could cost us dearly. Stay focused and follow the plan exactly."

The operation begins in the dead of night, the plane landing discreetly on a secluded airstrip outside Lillehammer. The biting cold only heightens the tension, our breaths forming clouds of vapor in the frigid air. We disembark silently, our footsteps barely audible on the snowy ground. The deserted streets provide perfect cover, but the danger is ever-present. Salameh's location is confirmed in a modest building, far from prying eyes. The team moves with military precision, every movement calculated to avoid detection. The dark corridors and narrow elevators become potential traps, but our resolve drives us forward despite the obstacles.

Suddenly, a door bursts open, and Salameh appears, flanked by bodyguards. My heart races, but I remain impassive, my face frozen like a marble statue. The exchange is swift and brutal, a silent confrontation where every gesture is critical.

"Take him down," David orders, his voice breaking the tension of the moment.

Shots ring out in the darkness, bullets slicing through the icy air. The operation descends into chaos, the attempt to capture Salameh turning into an uncontrolled firefight. The gunfire, muffled screams, and the piercing sound of bullets echo through the deserted streets, transforming Lillehammer into an unexpected battlefield. In the confusion, a fatal mistake occurs. An agent accidentally shoots an innocent civilian, a young man caught in the wrong place at the wrong time. The silence that follows the violence is suffocating, a crushing weight of guilt and impotence settling over us.

"What have we done?" Amir murmurs, his voice broken by the horror of the moment.

David, usually so composed, is overtaken by a silent fury.

"We must deal with this immediately," he orders, his voice trembling with restrained emotion. "Erase every trace. Neutralize any connection to this event."

The consequences of this blunder are devastating for Mossad. The organization's already fragile reputation is shattered by this tragedy. Internal discussions intensify, filled with accusations and doubts about our methods. Our mission of justice has morphed into a spiral of guilt and moral reckoning, leaving each agent to confront their own inner demons.

For me, the Lillehammer Affair leaves an indelible mark on my psyche. Visions of the young man caught in the crossfire haunt my nights, a persistent guilt that refuses to fade. The quest for vengeance, ignited after Munich, now collides with the harsh realities of its own consequences. Moral dilemmas deepen, each elimination mission becoming a test of my own humanity and my ability to justify my actions.

"We failed," David admits during a late-night meeting, his dark gaze fixed on the damning reports before him. "This mistake is costing us more than we ever imagined. We need to rethink our approach."

Discussions grow more critical, with heated debates about the legitimacy of our actions. Mossad agents, once united by a common determination, begin to feel the cracks of a deteriorating morality. The memories of Munich, mixed with those of Lillehammer, create a mosaic of pain and regret that prevents us from finding a clear consensus on the path forward.

For me, this period is a descent into the abyss of guilt and responsibility. Each failed mission or mistake serves as a reminder of the fragility of our quest for justice. Doubts creep in, forcing me to question the morality of our actions and the true nature of our mission. Vengeance, once seen as an act of justice, becomes an invisible chain binding me to a spiral of remorse and deep introspection.

As weeks turn into months, the Lillehammer Affair remains etched in our memories as a grim reminder of the limits of our organization and our humanity. Mossad, once seen as invincible, now finds itself confronting its own weaknesses and the need to reassess its methods. Introspective conversations and contemplative silences become commonplace, with each agent searching for a form of redemption amidst the chaos of their own thoughts.

Walking through the streets of Tel Aviv, I feel the weight of this operation on my shoulders, an invisible but ever-present burden that constantly reminds me of past mistakes. The Lillehammer Affair not only shook Mossad's reputation but also left an indelible mark on my conscience. The memories of this tragedy, combined with those of Munich, prevent me from finding inner peace, pushing me to seek a fragile balance between duty and humanity.

As I gaze at the shimmering lights of Tel Aviv from my office, I realize how much this operation has changed our approach to terrorism. The quest for vengeance has turned into a deep reflection on our own limits and the consequences of our actions. Mossad, while still determined to protect our nation, must now navigate the murky waters of morality and responsibility, seeking a balance between efficiency and humanity.

The Lillehammer Affair remains a dark chapter in our history, a bitter lesson on the dangers of vengeance and the moral challenges inherent in our mission. As a Mossad agent, I now face a more complex reality, where every action is a compromise between justice and guilt. And as the days pass, I know that this operation continues to shape our organization and my own existence, driving me to seek personal redemption amidst the shadows of our secret legend.

«Top Secret» Operations from 1948 to Today

The Secret History of Mossad

Chapter X

The Hunt for Salameh

Dawn breaks over Beirut, painting the sky a pale pink that contrasts sharply with the darkness of our intentions. The city, still ravaged by the chaos of civil war, is a labyrinth of shadows and mysteries. Every corner, every alley whispers buried secrets, a territory where each step could be a deadly trap. It is in this unstable landscape that our obsessive quest begins: the hunt for Ali Hassan Salameh, Yasser Arafat's right-hand man and a key figure in the PLO.

Sitting in a crowded café in Beirut, surrounded by the animated chatter of locals and the spicy scent of kebabs, I scan every face, searching for someone who might be watching me. Infiltrations in Lebanon are not mere missions; they are deep dives into a sea of unpredictable dangers. The efforts to locate Salameh are like a treasure hunt, with every clue becoming a precious piece of the puzzle that would lead us closer to our target.

"We need to stay even more vigilant," murmurs Amir, our counterintelligence specialist, as he subtly grazes his tea cup. His eyes scan the horizon as though they can pierce through Beirut's deepest secrets.

Infiltrations in Lebanon require the patience of a monk and the tenacity of a bear. Each mission is a delicate dance between discretion and swift action, where one wrong step could mean our downfall. Hostile environments—neighborhoods torn apart by violence and militia strongholds—are treacherous grounds where our determination is tested daily. Days blend into sleepless nights, marked by unexpected encounters and moments of quiet doubt. One evening, as the rain pounds against the windows of our temporary apartment, I receive an anonymous call. The voice on the other end is raspy, laden with nerves.

"We know you're hunting Salameh," the voice says in a low tone. "He's hiding in the Hamra district. Be careful—he's heavily protected."

My heart tightens. This information could be the key to our quest, but it could also be a trap set by our enemies. The moral dilemmas pile up, each decision weighing heavily on my conscience. The hunt for Salameh becomes an obsession, a fixation that consumes my thoughts and fuels an implacable determination.

"We need to quietly verify this information," says David, our mission leader, his piercing gaze betraying his calculated coldness. "Let's assemble an infiltration team and confirm his presence before we act."

The preparation for the operation becomes a race against time. Nights are filled with detailed plans, each step reviewed with almost paranoid meticulousness. The agents selected for the infiltration are chosen for their expertise and ability to blend into this dangerous environment. Tension rises as the operation date approaches, each second a drop in the already overflowing vase of stress.

On the day of the operation, the atmosphere is electric. The streets of Hamra, usually vibrant and colorful, are strangely calm, as if the city itself is holding its breath, waiting for the conclusion of our mission. We move with feline discretion, each step measured and every motion orchestrated to avoid drawing attention. The suspicious glances of passersby only amplify the suspense, each encounter testing the limits of our cover.

"It's here," David whispers, pointing to a discreet door behind which Salameh's apartment is supposedly located. "Stay ready. Once inside, follow the plan exactly."

We enter the apartment with military precision, our hearts pounding but our movements fluid and calculated. The scene inside is tense—Salameh is surrounded by his bodyguards, visibly suspicious but unaware of our actual presence. Adrenaline surges through me, every fiber of my being on high alert.

"It's now or never," Amir murmurs as we silently close in on our target.

The operation unfolds with lightning speed, every gesture a deadly dance between life and death. The exchanges are brief but intense—a silent struggle where each move counts. Salameh tries to flee, but our preparation and resolve prevail, neutralizing him before he can fully react. The mission's success is undeniable, but it leaves an indelible mark on our consciences. The return to Tel Aviv is just as delicate, requiring absolute discretion to avoid triggering an international incident. Reactions in Israel are swift—a wave of relief and pride sweeps over us—but the guilt over what we had to do lingers like a silent shadow.

The impact of this operation on Mossad is profound, strengthening our reputation while forcing us to confront the moral realities of our actions. For me, the hunt for Salameh became an obsession, a quest that surpassed mere duty and transformed into a personal mission for justice. The moments of suspense and hostile environments only deepened this fixation, with each success adding another stone to the edifice of our secret legend. Yet the moral questions persist, pushing me to reflect on the limits of our actions and the true nature of the justice we pursue.

"We did what had to be done," David says during the debriefing, his gaze fixed on the gathered intelligence. "But we must stay vigilant. The hunt never ends as long as the threat remains."

The challenges we faced during this hunt were just a prelude to the even more complex missions ahead.

The pursuit of Salameh strengthened our resolve but also left a deep imprint on our souls, with each successful mission tinged by an undercurrent of guilt and introspection. As a Mossad agent, I am now confronted with a reality where every victory is a blend of pride and questioning—a constant duality between duty and humanity.

Gazing at the shimmering lights of Tel Aviv from my office, I realize how much this hunt has shaped my life and career. The pursuit of an elusive enemy has become a metaphor for my own internal struggle— an endless battle to find balance between justice and guilt. Mossad, with its relentless determination and fearsome efficiency, continues to evolve, ready to face new threats with the same intensity and obsession that led us to capture Salameh. And I, too, am ready to continue the hunt, knowing that every step forward is a victory, but also a confrontation with my own inner demons.

The Secret History of Mossad

Chapter XI

Doubts and Controversies

The shadow of past operations looms heavily within the austere walls of Mossad. Since Munich, murmurs of disapproval and worried glances have infiltrated the corridors, weaving a web of doubt and questioning that extends far beyond our daily missions. As an agent of this secret organization, I find myself in deep introspection, silently questioning the methods we employ to protect our nation. Sitting in a dimly lit meeting room, I scrutinize the familiar faces of my colleagues. Ethical debates have become commonplace, each discussion a battle between duty and morality. David, our deputy director, opens the session with an unusual gravity.

— We need to discuss the repercussions of our recent operations, — he begins, his voice laden with fatigue and seriousness. — The methods we use are raising legitimate questions within our team.

Amir, our cryptography specialist, speaks up, his words hanging heavily in the stagnant air of the room.

— Are we crossing a line from which we cannot

return, — he questions, his gaze lost in the void. — Each elimination mission, each sabotage operation, pulls us further from our initial principles.

I feel a weight settle on my shoulders. The elimination missions, once seen as acts of necessary justice, are beginning to morph into a spiral of guilt and moral doubt. Tensions between agents are palpable, the exchanges growing more tense, each diverging opinion adding another layer to our collective dilemma.

— We are supposed to protect our people, — asserts Yitzhak, a seasoned agent, his voice tinged with frustration. — But at what cost? Every time we eliminate an enemy, we also lose a part of our humanity.

Yitzhak's words resonate deeply within me, awakening an acute awareness of the fragility of our mission. Personal reflections on justice and vengeance multiply, each completed operation becoming another brick in the edifice of our secret legend, but also a heavy burden on our souls. In moments of solitude, I can't help but wonder if our actions are truly justified. The line between right and wrong grows increasingly blurry, each mission pushing us to navigate the murky waters of morality. The memories of the innocent faces lost during our failed operations haunt my thoughts, a painful reminder of the unforeseen consequences of our actions. One evening, after a long day of failed missions and internal debates, I find myself alone in my office, the weight of responsibility crushing my chest. I stare at photographs from past missions, each image

a window into difficult choices and personal sacrifices. The loneliness of a Mossad agent becomes more
palpable than ever, each decision a constant struggle
between duty and conscience.

— We cannot ignore these feelings, — Amir
murmurs as he discreetly enters my office, his presence
calming but marked by concern. — We must find a
balance between our mission and our humanity.

I look up, recognizing his silent support. The
internal discussions within Mossad are transforming
into a collective quest for meaning, an attempt to
reconcile our actions with our personal values. Moral
dilemmas are omnipresent, each agent seeking to
understand where the line lies between protecting our
nation and preserving our moral integrity.

— How can we continue to protect Israel without
losing our soul, — he asks, his voice filled with sincerity. — How do we justify our actions in the face of
human consequences?

These questions haunt me, each answer seeming to
push us further from our initial ideals. Tensions within
the team rise, debates sometimes becoming heated,
each person defending their own convictions about the
best way to carry out our mission. The camaraderie of
the past is now tinged with skepticism and remorse,
a silent but profound transformation that calls into
question the very cohesion of our organization. I recall
conversations with David, where strategic decisions are
now intertwined with deep reflections on the ethical

implications of our actions. Each completed mission is a tactical victory but also a source of silent guilt that simmers within me, threatening to undermine my determination and faith in our mission.

— We must continue to protect our people, — David reaffirms during a particularly tense meeting. — But we must also be aware of the consequences of our actions. It's time to reassess our methods and find a balance between effectiveness and morality.

David's words mark the beginning of a new era of reflection within Mossad, an attempt to reconcile our duty with our human values. The debates become more constructive, each agent bringing their own perspectives and moral dilemmas to the discussion table. The search for ethical solutions becomes a common goal, an effort to maintain our integrity while ensuring the security of our nation. For my part, these internal controversies drive me to deep introspection. The doubts that have been haunting me grow more insidious, questioning the legitimacy of our actions and the true nature of our mission. Personal reflections on justice and vengeance evolve into a quest for meaning, an attempt to understand how to navigate the complex landscape of morality while remaining true to our duty to Israel. As the weeks turn into months, the internal controversies within Mossad persist, but they also become a source of renewal and strengthening. The search for a balance between effectiveness and ethics pushes us to innovate, to rethink our methods, and to reinforce our team's cohesion. Introspective discussions and moments of personal reflection become essential parts of our daily lives, an effort to preserve our humanity in the face of the relentless challenges of our mission.

Reflecting on past events and current debates, I realize how crucial this period of doubts and controversies is for our evolution as an organization and as individuals. Mossad, once a force united by a common determination, now faces its own limits and the need to rethink its methods to remain relevant and effective in a constantly changing world. The road is long and fraught with obstacles, but the quest for a balance between our mission and our moral integrity is an essential struggle to ensure the survival and prosperity of our nation without sacrificing our humanity. Each reflection, each debate, is a stone added to the edifice of our secret legend, a legend that must remain true to its values while evolving in the face of the relentless challenges of the modern world. As I close my eyes and let my thoughts wander, I feel both exhausted and determined. Doubts and controversies are not obstacles, but catalysts for change, essential elements for forging a strong and resilient organization. Mossad, with its relentless quest for justice and security, continues to evolve, ready to face future challenges with heightened awareness and renewed determination.

The Secret History of Mossad

Chapter XII

The Osirak Reactor

The winter of 1981 descends on Paris with implacable rigor, wrapping the City of Light in a shroud of gloom and biting cold. The once lively streets are cloaked in a heavy silence, an atmosphere ripe for the clandestine operations unfolding in the shadows of historic buildings. It is against this austere backdrop that a mission of utmost importance takes place: preventing Iraq from acquiring a nuclear weapon, a threat that weighs heavily on regional and global stability. Seated in the Mossad briefing room, surrounded by strategic maps and detailed reports, I feel the adrenaline surge. David, our deputy director, unfolds a series of meticulously prepared plans before us. His precise movements reflect the complexity of the operation ahead, each detail scrutinized with obsessive attention.

— The Osirak reactor in Iraq poses a direct threat to the security of our nation, — he declares gravely. — If we do not neutralize this facility, the consequences could be catastrophic.

The murmurs in the room blend worry with determination. Previous sabotage attempts have already been numerous, but each was met with insurmountable obstacles. Diplomatic pressures are intensifying, alliances are tightening, and geopolitical tensions are reaching their peak. It is clear that direct action is now inevitable, and we must act with surgical precision to avoid any failure. The recruitment of the pilot is a crucial step in our plan. We need a trusted man, capable of navigating the murky waters of espionage and successfully carrying out such a perilous mission. After weeks of searching and discreet infiltrations, we have identified a potential candidate: Captain Eliav Cohen, an experienced pilot with an impeccable military background and unwavering loyalty to Israel.

— Eliav is our best asset, — affirms Amir, our counter-espionage specialist. — His deep knowledge of aerial tactics and ability to operate under pressure make him the ideal candidate for this mission.

The delicate negotiations with Eliav are a complex dance between trust and manipulation. We must gain his trust without raising suspicion, offering him a sufficiently powerful motivation to risk his life for our cause. Meetings multiply, each interaction adding another piece to the puzzle we need to assemble to finalize our plan. The preparations for the operation are intense and demanding. Every step is orchestrated with military precision, each detail reviewed and re-reviewed to minimize risks and maximize the chances of success. Internal discussions follow one another, strategies are drawn and readjusted according to the latest intelligence. Coordination between teams is essential, each agent playing a specific role in this clandestine ballet where a single mistake could cost dearly. One evening, as the lights of Paris twinkle in the distance, I find myself alone in my office, reflecting on the implications of our mission. The responsibility weighs heavily on my shoulders, and doubts begin to creep into my mind. Are we doing the right thing by intervening directly? The potential consequences of this operation are immense, not only for our national security but also for the global geopolitical balance.

— You seem thoughtful, — Yitzhak, a trusted colleague, suddenly remarks, entering the room discreetly. — Is everything all right?

I look up, trying to hide my worries. — It's a delicate mission, — I respond with a forced smile. — But we must do what is necessary to protect our nation.

The days pass, and the date of the operation draws near. Excitement and tension blend, creating an electric atmosphere within our team. Final checks are carried out, equipment is prepared, and plans are refined with almost obsessive meticulousness. Every detail is reviewed to ensure that nothing will hinder our mission, every contingency planned for to handle the unexpected. On D-Day, dawn breaks over a silent Paris. Final preparations are carried out with ruthless efficiency, each agent in place, ready to execute their role with military precision. We gather in our secret base, an underground facility beneath the city streets, and one last time, we review the action plan.

— Remember, — David declares, his gaze fixed on each of us, — discretion is our most valuable ally. Our actions must remain invisible to the enemy, but their impact will be significant.

The minutes tick by, each second seeming to stretch into infinity. The tension is palpable, the air charged with an electric energy that resonates through the room. Agents exchange determined glances, aware of the importance of what is about to happen. The sabotage operation must be executed with surgical precision, each movement a delicate dance between efficiency and discretion. We move stealthily toward the Osirak site, avoiding enemy patrols and using ingenious subterfuge to remain unnoticed. The hostile environment is unforgiving, every step a struggle against fatigue and fear. The challenges are numerous, but our determination is unshakable. Internal discussions with Eliav are brief but crucial, each instruction delivered with deadly clarity and precision.

— Everything must go as planned, — David murmurs as we approach the reactor. — We cannot afford a mistake.

The operation begins with lightning speed. Explosives are placed with surgical precision, each detonation calculated to maximize the impact on the nuclear facilities without drawing immediate attention.

Agents carry out their tasks with ruthless efficiency, every movement a demonstration of our expertise and determination. The impact of this operation on the geopolitical balance is immediate and profound. The United Nations responds swiftly, imposing severe economic sanctions on Iraq and tightening controls on nuclear facilities in the region. Diplomatic pressure intensifies, alliances tighten, and regional tensions reach their zenith. With this audacious operation, Mossad positions itself as a formidable and respected force on the global stage. For me, this mission marks a major turning point in my career. The success of this sabotage operation has not only strengthened our strategic position but also marked a crucial step in our fight against nuclear threats. The emotions felt upon seeing the results of our work are a complex mix of pride and relief, but also a sharp awareness of the increased responsibilities that now lie upon us.

The fallout from the operation is felt far beyond our nation's borders. International relations are redefined, alliances are strengthened, and the geopolitical landscape is forever altered. Mossad, with its ingenuity and determination, becomes an indispensable figure in the fight against nuclear proliferation, a secret legend whose impact resonates across the globe. However, this success is not without its own challenges. Internal and external pressures mount, expectations growing ever higher as we consolidate our position. Ethical debates multiply, each completed mission offering a new opportunity to question our methods and motivations. The balance between efficiency and morality becomes a constant struggle, each decision an attempt to find a fragile equilibrium between protecting our nation and preserving our moral integrity. As I contemplate the bustling streets of Tel Aviv from my office, I realize how much this operation has changed our approach to intelligence and sabotage. The Osirak reactor is not only a military victory but also a profound lesson on the limits of our power and the responsibilities that come with it. Mossad, as an organization, continues to evolve, adapting its strategies to anticipate and neutralize emerging threats with the same determination and verbal agility that allowed us to triumph in this historic mission. For my part, this operation strengthens my conviction in our mission, but it also pushes me toward deeper reflection on the nature of justice and the sacrifices necessary to preserve it. Each completed mission is a silent victory, but it also leaves an indelible mark on my mind, constantly reminding me of why we do what we do and what the consequences are.

As the days pass and the geopolitical balance continues to shift, I know that our mission is only just beginning. The Osirak reactor is a cornerstone of our fight against nuclear proliferation, but it is also a symbol of the relentless challenges that lie ahead. As a Mossad agent, I am ready to face these challenges with the same determination and vigilance, aware that each completed mission brings us closer to our ultimate goal: ensuring the survival and prosperity of the State of Israel in an ever-changing world.

The Secret History of Mossad

Chapter XIII

The Iranian Enemy

The winter of 1983 marks a decisive turning point in Middle Eastern geopolitics. Iran, after decades of tensions, emerges as a new nuclear threat, its ambitions driven by an unyielding desire to upend the regional balance. The news reverberates through the quiet halls of Mossad, stirring a persistent yet silent sense of concern. I stand at the center of this storm, fully aware that every decision made today could shape the future of our nation. Discussions within Mossad have become more intense, each agent weighing the implications of such a threat. David, our deputy director, outlines the gravity of the situation with alarming clarity.

— Iran is not merely threatening our security, — he asserts, his eyes scanning the room with fierce determination. — They are aiming to acquire a nuclear capability that could disrupt the balance of power in the region.

The challenges posed by this newly identified enemy are numerous and complex. Iran, fortified by shifting alliances and an extensive network of influence, represents an insidious threat. Previous attempts at sabotage and infiltration have revealed an organization fiercely determined to achieve its goals at any cost. The emergence of this nuclear threat demands a complete reevaluation of our strategies and a rapid adaptation to an ever-evolving geopolitical landscape. My personal involvement in this dossier intensifies as the weeks go by. Nights stretch into endless vigils, filled with meticulous analyses and strategic meetings. Each report, each piece of intelligence gathered, is a part of the complex puzzle we must assemble to anticipate Iran's movements. Adrenaline and tension have become my constant companions, every decision weighing heavily on my conscience.

— We need to anticipate their moves before they can realize their ambitions, — declares Amir, our cryptology specialist, during a late-night meeting. — Information is our most powerful weapon. Without it, we are blind to their intentions.

His words resonate within me, underscoring the crucial importance of intelligence in our fight against this new threat. Diplomatic pressures are intensifying, traditional alliances are being redefined, and international tensions are reaching dizzying heights. Iran, with its belligerent rhetoric and nuclear ambitions, has become the center of a complex web of rivalries and conspiracies. Infiltrations into the heart of Iran prove to be perilous missions, where every step is a dance with death. The hostile environments, from underground laboratories to fortified military bases, are minefields where a single mistake can be costly. The subterfuge employed to remain unnoticed multiplies, turning our daily lives into a series of meticulously orchestrated disguises and deceptions. Each mission is a test of our ingenuity and determination, a constant struggle to obtain crucial information without arousing suspicion. One evening, as I return home after an exhausting day, the twinkling lights of Tel Aviv seem distant and unreal. Personal reflections on justice and vengeance mix with a deep melancholy. The quest to neutralize the Iranian threat has become an obsession, a fixation that consumes my thoughts and fuels an unwavering determination. Yet, behind this façade of resilience, silent doubts begin to creep in, questioning the morality of our actions and the legitimacy of our mission.

— You seem troubled, — Yitzhak, a trusted colleague, suddenly remarks as he discreetly enters my apartment. — Is everything all right?

I look up, trying to mask my inner turmoil. — Yes, — I reply with a forced smile. — Just a lot to think about.

Ethical debates within Mossad have become commonplace, each elimination mission a brutal reminder of the limits of our power and the fragility of our humanity. Tensions among the agents are palpable, each person defending their own convictions about the best way to carry out our mission. Discussions turn into silent battles, where loyalty to our nation clashes with individual conscience.

— We do what we must to protect our people, — David asserts during a tense meeting, his determined gaze fixed on each member of the team. — But we must also remain vigilant about the consequences of our actions. The line between justice and vengeance is thin, and we cannot afford to cross it irreversibly.

His words echo the moral dilemmas that haunt every Mossad agent. Personal reflections on the complexity of this nuclear threat multiply, each completed mission another stone added to the edifice of our secret legend, but also a heavy burden on our souls. The hunt for Salameh, the Osirak operation—each successful mission brings us closer to our goal, but it also pulls us further away from our initial ideals. The impact of this operation on the geopolitical balance is deep and immediate. Alliances are strengthened and redefined, regional tensions multiply, and international pressures intensify. Iran, with its nuclear ambitions, is now at the heart of a complex network of rivalries that threatens to plunge the region into devastating conflict. Mossad, as a strategic intelligence body, plays a crucial role in this silent struggle, but the shadow of our own actions begins to obscure our clear and determined vision. For me, this period is a descent into the abyss of morality and responsibility. The doubts that had been brewing inside me grow stronger, pushing me to reflect deeply on the true nature of our mission. The quest to neutralize the Iranian threat has become an internal struggle, a battle between duty and humanity. Each completed mission is a strategic victory, but it is also a moral ordeal that calls into question the legitimacy of our actions and the true meaning of the justice we seek.

As months turn into years, Iran continues to evolve as a formidable enemy, its nuclear ambitions advancing despite our relentless efforts to thwart them. Strategic changes within Mossad are necessary, adapting our methods and strengthening our capabilities to face this complex threat. Infiltration and sabotage missions multiply, each operation an attempt to slow Iran's nuclear progress without provoking uncontrolled escalation. Reflecting on past events and the challenges ahead, I realize how much this Iranian threat has transformed our organization and our very existence as Mossad agents. The complexity of this threat, coupled with growing international tensions, demands constant adaptation and deep reflection on our methods and motivations. The quest to neutralize a nuclear Iran is an unending mission, a relentless struggle to maintain balance and ensure the survival of our nation in an ever-changing world. As I gaze at the distant lights of Tel Aviv, I know that our mission continues, fueled by the same determination and vigilance that have always defined us. Iran, with its nuclear ambitions, remains a complex and determined threat, but Mossad, with its resilience and ingenuity, is ready to face the challenges ahead. And I, as an agent of this legendary organization, am ready to pursue this quest with the same determination and moral awareness, knowing that each completed mission brings us closer to our ultimate goal: ensuring the security and prosperity of the State of Israel in an uncertain and often hostile world.

«Top Secret» Operations from 1948 to Today

Chapter XIV

Sabotage and Sanctions

The winter of 1985 plunges Iran into a freezing darkness, reflecting the turmoil that grips the country. The Iranian nuclear program, long hidden in the darkest corners of industrial and military facilities, has become a palpable threat to regional stability. In this climate of heightened tension, Mossad intensifies its sabotage operations, determined to curb Iran's nuclear ambitions before they materialize into a devastating weapon. Seated in the command center's meeting room, I scrutinize the geographical maps spread out before me, each line and mark representing a crucial piece of our strategy. David, our deputy director, lays out a detailed plan on the whiteboard, his precise gestures emphasizing the importance of each step.

— We must act swiftly and discreetly, — he declares gravely. — Time is running out, and every day counts to prevent Iran from crossing the red line towards nuclear armament.

The sabotage operations are orchestrated with surgical precision, each mission designed to strike at the heart of Iran's nuclear program without leaving a trace. The methods employed vary, ranging from silent infiltration of facilities to the use of sophisticated explosive devices and hacking into computer systems to sow chaos in critical databases. Each action is a piece of the strategic puzzle, aimed at slowing, disrupting, and ultimately stopping Iran's nuclear development.

— Our field agents have identified several key targets, — explains Amir, our technology and cyber-operations specialist, adjusting his glasses. — The reactors, centrifuge factories, and research centers are our top priorities. We need to neutralize them without triggering a major international reaction.

The risks involved are immense. Each sabotage operation is a delicate dance between efficiency and discretion, where the slightest mistake could not only compromise the mission but also endanger the lives of infiltrated agents and trigger an escalation of diplomatic tensions. Diplomatic pressures are mounting, the economic sanctions imposed by the international community further isolating Iran, and regional tensions are reaching dizzying heights. I particularly recall the «Silent Storm» mission, a daring operation aimed at destroying a clandestine centrifuge facility in the Iranian desert. The team, composed of expert technicians and infiltrated agents, had to navigate through a hostile landscape, where every step was a battle against crushing heat and Iranian security forces. The mission was a resounding success, but it left deep scars, both physical and psychological, on those who participated.

— It was a high-risk operation, but we managed to destroy the facility without alerting the Iranian authorities, — David confides during our post-mission debriefing. — It's a strategic victory, but we must remain vigilant. Iran will redouble its efforts to rebuild what they've lost.

The economic sanctions imposed on Iran have had a significant impact on its economy, considerably slowing its progress in the nuclear field. Imports of critical materials have become more difficult, and exports of strategic products are severely restricted. However, Iran has found ingenious ways to bypass these obstacles, relying on clandestine networks and improbable alliances to keep its program alive. International tensions have intensified, with each country taking sides in this geopolitical chess game. Israel's allies applaud our efforts, but the international community remains divided, with some countries criticizing our methods and direct interventions. Diplomatic dialogues grow increasingly tense, with each sabotage operation closely watched by international observers.

— We must stay the course, — declares Amir during a strategic meeting, his determined gaze fixed on the map projected before him. — Iran is a real and present threat. Our actions are necessary to ensure the security of our nation and our allies.

Anecdotes about specific missions abound, each illustrating the unique challenges and moments of suspense that punctuate our fight against Iran. I remember the «Scarlet Night» mission, where we infiltrated a research laboratory under the guise of a maintenance team. Tensions were high, with every minute testing our patience and precision. The discovery of detailed reactor plans was a major breakthrough, allowing us to plan more targeted and effective operations.

— We need this information to anticipate their next steps, — David explains, his grave tone underscoring the importance of each discovery. — Every detail we obtain gives us a crucial strategic advantage.

Covert missions in France have become an essential component of our global strategy. Embassies, universities, and research centers are infiltrated by our agents, each playing a key role in gathering vital information. The challenges are numerous, from constant surveillance to managing multiple identities, with every operation a constant battle against detection and failure. My personal involvement in this dossier runs deep and committed. Each completed mission strengthens my determination, but it also fuels a growing obsession to neutralize this Iranian threat. Sleepless nights spent analyzing data, intense discussions with colleagues, and personal reflections on justice and vengeance follow one another, shaping my vision and commitment to our mission.

— We're at a critical juncture, — Amir asserts during a late-night meeting, his serious gaze fixed on the data screens. — Every successful operation brings us closer to our goal, but it also increases the risks and challenges we must overcome.

The feelings surrounding these operations are a complex mix of pride, fear, and guilt. The satisfaction of having helped slow down a potentially devastating nuclear program is tainted by the awareness of the human lives put at risk and the personal sacrifices required to complete our missions. Moral dilemmas are omnipresent, with every action a compromise between strategic effectiveness and moral integrity.

— We do what we must to protect our nation, — David declares during a debriefing meeting, his tone marked by unwavering determination. — But we must also remain aware of the limits of our methods and the implications of our actions.

Personal reflections on the complexity of this threat and the growing international tensions intertwine, creating a dark and contemplative backdrop to our relentless fight against a nuclear Iran. The methods employed, though technical and precise, are constantly questioned by the ethical and moral challenges we face. The balance between strategic necessity and personal morality is a daily struggle, with each agent having to find their own equilibrium between duty and humanity. As I reflect on the fallout of our actions on the geopolitical balance, I realize how our fight against a nuclear Iran is an endless quest, a battle where each victory is both a step forward and a new source of challenges. The sabotage operations and imposed sanctions have weakened Iran's nuclear program, but they have also intensified regional and international tensions, creating an atmosphere of mistrust and heightened rivalry.

For me, this period is a total immersion into the depths of strategy and morality. The challenges posed by a nuclear Iran are immense, but they also strengthen our determination and resilience as Mossad agents. Each completed mission is another stone added to the edifice of our secret legend, a legend built on sacrifices, courage, and an unwavering will to protect our nation. As I walk the bustling streets of Tel Aviv after a long day of missions, I feel a mix of pride and deep reflection. The sabotage operations and sanctions imposed on Iran are acts of silent warfare, demonstrations of our ingenuity and determination to prevent a nuclear catastrophe. But they are also constant reminders of the moral dilemmas and personal sacrifices inherent in our mission. Mossad, with its technical methods and sophisticated strategies, continues to evolve to face this complex threat. International tensions continue to rise, and each operation is an attempt to maintain the fragile balance between national security and regional stability. My personal commitment to this mission is stronger than ever, fueled by an unwavering determination to protect our nation and ensure the survival of the State of Israel in the face of persistent and evolving threats.

«Top Secret» Operations from 1948 to Today

The Secret History of Mossad

Chapter XV

The Cyber War

The dawn of 2010 ushers in a new era, where war is no longer fought solely on the battlefield but also in the invisible realms of cyberspace. The skyscrapers of Tel Aviv glisten under the first rays of the sun, a reflection of a nation resolved to defend its sovereignty through innovative yet perilous means. In this rapidly advancing technological landscape, Mossad embraces a new form of warfare: cyber operations, symbolized by the infamous Stuxnet virus. Sitting in the ultra-secure briefing room, surrounded by my team of computer and engineering experts, I feel a mix of excitement and apprehension. David, our deputy director, outlines the contours of this revolutionary digital weapon before us.

— Stuxnet is not just malware, — he begins, his eyes gleaming with fierce determination. — It's a precision weapon designed to infiltrate and disrupt Iranian nuclear infrastructures with unmatched discretion.

Technical explanations fly around the room, each word resonating like a note in this clandestine symphony. Amir, our cryptology specialist, details the sophisticated mechanisms of the virus, using precise but accessible language.

— Stuxnet exploits multiple zero-day vulnerabilities, — he explains. — It's programmed to specifically target the SCADA systems used in Natanz's centrifuges, disrupting their operation without leaving an immediate trace.

The development of Stuxnet is a technological marvel, the result of close collaborations between the brightest minds at Mossad and international partners. Intense discussions with cybersecurity and software engineering experts multiply, each idea scrutinized and refined to ensure maximum effectiveness. Sleepless nights spent coding and testing the virus testify to the unwavering commitment of our team, ready to do whatever it takes to neutralize this nuclear threat. The challenges faced during this mission are numerous and complex. The need to bypass Iran's advanced security systems demands unprecedented ingenuity. Every infiltration attempt must be meticulously planned, each step executed with surgical precision. The risks of being detected are ever-present, but the determination to protect our nation far outweighs the fear of failure. Diplomatic pressures add another layer of complexity, with every clandestine action a delicate dance between operational effectiveness and strategic discretion.

One particularly memorable anecdote from this mission remains etched in my memory. During an infiltration of an Iranian research center, our team had to bypass a series of sophisticated firewalls and advanced detection systems. The tension was palpable, each click and line of code a test of patience and technical mastery. Finally, after hours of intense effort, we succeeded in introducing Stuxnet into the system, triggering a series of silent but devastating malfunctions in the nuclear centrifuges.

— It's done, — Amir announced, a tired but satisfied smile spreading across his face. — The virus is active. Now, we need to closely monitor the system's reactions.

The effects of Stuxnet on Iran's nuclear program are immediate and profound. The centrifuges begin to malfunction, causing delays and significant losses in enriched uranium production. Iranian engineers, baffled by these unexplained failures, are unable to pinpoint the real cause, allowing Mossad to operate in the shadows with ruthless efficiency. This digital sabotage operation marks a turning point in the fight against nuclear proliferation, demonstrating the power of cyber operations as tools of strategic warfare.

However, this victory is not without consequences. International reactions are mixed, ranging from tacit admiration to veiled suspicion. Israel's allies commend our ingenuity, while our adversaries wonder how such an operation could have been carried out with such discretion. Geopolitical tensions intensify, with each country adjusting its alliances and strategies in the face of this new form of invisible yet highly effective warfare. Personally, my involvement in this cyber-sabotage mission has profoundly impacted my perception of war and national security. The ability to manipulate complex systems remotely, to cause invisible but devastating disruptions, opens a new dimension in our strategic arsenal. Yet this new form of warfare also raises ethical and moral questions, challenging the boundary between defense and aggression.

— Are we crossing a line from which we can't return, — Amir sometimes asks me during our informal discussions, his piercing gaze reflecting a shared concern. — Stuxnet is a powerful weapon, but it carries the risk of setting dangerous precedents.

These reflections haunt me, with every success in cyberspace a strategic victory but also a source of inner doubts. The ease with which a digital weapon can be deployed raises questions about the limits of our power and the unforeseen consequences of our actions. The determination to protect our nation clashes with the awareness of potential collateral damage, creating a constant duality between duty and morality.

The tense scenes encountered during sabotage missions are intense physical and mental trials. The pressure to maintain discretion while executing complex operations demands unwavering resilience and concentration. Hostile environments, from clandestine research labs to militarized control centers, are minefields where every move must be calculated with extreme precision. The technical challenges, such as countermeasures implemented by Iran to detect and neutralize our cyber-attacks, are constant and require rapid adaptation and continuous innovation.

One particularly trying moment occurred during an attempt to update Stuxnet to bypass a new Iranian defense system. The stress and fatigue mounted, with each line of code a battle against time and the increasing complexity of the enemy's systems. The pressure was such that any mistake could not only compromise the operation but also expose the identity of our infiltrated agents. Yet the satisfaction of seeing our work bear fruit, as the Iranian centrifuges failed, was an invaluable reward that fueled our determination to continue this invisible but crucial fight.

The impact of this operation on the geopolitical balance is multifaceted and profound. Iran, weakened in its nuclear program, sees its ambitions slowed, while Israel's allies strengthen their support and cooperation in intelligence and cybersecurity. Regional tensions ease slightly, with the nuclear threat now contained, but the climate of mistrust and rivalry remains palpable. Mossad, with its cyber arsenal, becomes a formidable and respected force, an invisible but omnipresent shadow in the fight against nuclear threats.

For me, this cyber war represents a significant evolution in how we conceive and conduct intelligence operations. The ability to neutralize a nuclear threat remotely, without direct bloodshed, is a major technological advancement that redefines the scope of our mission. However, this new form of warfare also requires constant adaptation, a perpetual updating of our skills and strategies to stay ahead of emerging threats.

The collaborations necessary for the development and deployment of Stuxnet are also a crucial aspect of this operation. Working closely with international cybersecurity experts, software engineers, and intelligence analysts is a complex undertaking that requires smooth communication and flawless coordination. Each team member plays a specific role, contributing their unique expertise to the success of the mission. Trust and loyalty between agents are essential, with every operation a demonstration of our ability to work together toward a common goal.

Personal impressions of this new form of warfare are ambivalent. On the one hand, the pride in contributing to the protection of our nation through innovative and effective means is immense. On the other hand, the awareness of the ethical and moral implications of our actions creates a constant internal tension. The ease with which we can inflict invisible but devastating damage raises questions about the limits of our power and the responsibility that comes with it. This duality between strategic effectiveness and moral integrity is a daily struggle, a quest for meaning in an ever-evolving landscape of war.

One evening, as I gaze at the lights of Tel Aviv

from my office, I reflect on the scope of our actions. Stuxnet has proven that cyber warfare is an inescapable reality, a dimension of the struggle for supremacy that requires continuous vigilance and innovation. But this digital victory is also a lesson in the potential dangers of weapons.

Chapter XVI

Stuxnet: The Invisible Weapon

The dawn of 2010 arises over a world undergoing a technological transformation, where the boundaries of war blur, giving way to a silent and invisible battle. In this digital era, Mossad deploys a revolutionary weapon, the Stuxnet virus, symbolizing a conflict fought not by soldiers on the ground, but by elusive lines of code. This operation, both audacious and controversial, marks a crucial step in the evolution of intelligence and national security. Sitting in the ultra-secret control room, surrounded by my team of cyber-security and software engineering experts, I feel a mix of excitement and apprehension. David, our deputy director, unveils the operation plan with almost surgical precision.

— Stuxnet is not just malware, — he begins, his eyes gleaming with fierce determination. — It's a precision weapon designed to infiltrate and disrupt Iranian nuclear infrastructures without leaving visible traces.

Technical explanations flow around us, each word resonating like a note in this clandestine symphony. Amir, our cryptology specialist, details the virus's sophisticated mechanisms with precise yet accessible language.

— Stuxnet exploits multiple zero-day vulnerabilities, — he explains. — It's programmed to specifically target the SCADA systems used in Natanz's centrifuges, silently but devastatingly disrupting their operation.

The development of Stuxnet represents an unprecedented technological feat. Close collaborations with renowned computer engineers and international cybersecurity experts enabled the creation of a virus capable of navigating the intricate control systems of Iranian industrial infrastructures. Sleepless nights spent coding and testing the virus reflect our team's unwavering commitment, ready to do whatever it takes to neutralize this nuclear threat before it becomes irreversible. The challenges encountered during this mission are numerous and complex. Bypassing Iran's advanced security systems requires boundless ingenuity and constant adaptation. Every infiltration attempt must be meticulously planned, each step executed with military precision to avoid detection. The risks of being exposed are ever-present, but the determination to protect our nation far outweighs the fear of failure. Diplomatic pressures intensify, alliances tighten, and geopolitical tensions reach dizzying heights.

A memorable anecdote from this operation remains etched in my memory. During a covert infiltration mission at the heart of Natanz's facilities, our team had to navigate a labyrinth of control rooms and clandestine laboratories. The stress was at its peak, every step testing our patience and technical mastery. Suddenly, a silent alarm sounded, a subtle warning of a possible intrusion. Through a combination of tactical finesse and quick thinking, we managed to restore discretion, but the incident heightened our team's vigilance and effectiveness.

— This is an unprecedented operation, — David stated during our post-mission debriefing, his gaze fixed on the collected data. — We successfully infiltrated the system without triggering a major alarm. Now, we need to monitor the reactions and adjust our approach accordingly.

The effects of Stuxnet on Iran's nuclear program are immediate and profound. Natanz's centrifuges begin to malfunction, causing significant delays in enriched uranium production. Iranian engineers, puzzled by these unexplained malfunctions, are unable to determine the real cause, allowing Mossad to operate in the shadows with ruthless efficiency. This digital sabotage operation marks a turning point in the fight against nuclear proliferation, demonstrating the power of cyber operations as tools of strategic warfare.

However, this victory is not without its limits. Stuxnet, despite its initial effectiveness, also reveals its flaws and unforeseen consequences. The virus, designed to be precise, eventually spreads beyond its original target, infecting other industrial systems worldwide. This uncontrolled expansion raises ethical and technical questions, highlighting the inherent risks of using complex and potentially uncontrollable digital weapons. The Iranian regime's responses are varied and strategic. Initially, the government tries to conceal the malfunctions by claiming they are independent technical problems. However, savvy analysts begin to suspect external intervention, sowing distrust and paranoia among Iran's elites. Diplomatic pressures intensify, with each country attempting to understand the origin of this invisible yet devastating attack.

For me, involvement in this cyber-sabotage mission has profoundly impacted my perception of war and national security. The ability to manipulate complex systems remotely, to cause invisible but devastating malfunctions, opens a new dimension in our strategic arsenal. Yet, this new form of warfare also raises ethical and moral questions, challenging the boundary between defense and aggression.

— We've changed the game in the fight against nuclear weapons, — Amir asserts during a strategic meeting, his serious gaze fixed on the data screens. — But at what cost? Stuxnet's uncontrolled spread forces us to rethink our methods and anticipate the consequences of our actions.

These reflections haunt me, with every success in

cyberspace a strategic victory but also a source of inner doubts. The ease with which a digital weapon can be deployed raises questions about the limits of our power and the responsibilities that come with it. The determination to protect our nation clashes with the awareness of potential collateral damage, creating a constant duality between duty and morality.

The behind-the-scenes aspects of the Stuxnet operation are marked by relentless technical and logistical challenges. The necessary collaborations with international cybersecurity and software engineering experts are complex and demanding. Each team member brings unique expertise, contributing to the virus's design and deployment with ruthless efficiency. Technical discussions are often intense, with each idea scrutinized and refined to ensure maximum effectiveness while minimizing the risk of failure.

Another memorable anecdote concerns the testing phase of Stuxnet in a controlled environment. Initial results were promising, with the ability to disrupt SCADA systems in a targeted manner. However, simulations revealed potential flaws, forcing our team to rework the code and strengthen control mechanisms to prevent any uncontrolled spread. This stage was a crucial lesson in the limits and responsibilities inherent in creating sophisticated digital weapons.

— We must keep refining our approach, — David stated during a post-test review session. — Every improvement brings us closer to our goal, but it also reminds us of the potential dangers of our creations.

The challenges of waging an invisible war are numerous and complex. The discreet nature of cyber operations makes it difficult to precisely assess their effectiveness and real impacts. Sabotage missions, though successful, often leave ambiguous traces, making it impossible to clearly attribute responsibility. This strategic ambiguity is both a strength and a weakness, offering effective cover while exposing Mossad to potential accusations of digital aggression.

Yet, the evolution of intelligence into cyberspace is inevitable and essential in the modern world. Cyber operations like Stuxnet represent a major advance in our ability to defend our nation against asymmetric and technological threats. They testify to our ingenuity and ability to innovate in the face of unprecedented challenges, but they also raise crucial questions about ethics and responsibility in the use of cutting-edge technologies.

Reflecting on Stuxnet's fallout on the geopolitical balance, I realize how much this operation has redefined our approach to intelligence and national security. Iran, weakened in its nuclear program, sees its ambitions slowed, while Israel's allies strengthen their support and cooperation in intelligence and cybersecurity. Regional tensions ease slightly, with the nuclear threat now contained, but the climate of mistrust and rivalry remains palpable.

For me, this mission represents a pivotal moment

in my career and in Mossad's history. The success of Stuxnet has not only strengthened our strategic position, but it has also marked a defining moment in our fight against nuclear threats. The emotions felt when witnessing the results of our work are a complex mix of pride, relief, and acute awareness of the increased responsibilities that now rest upon us.

— We must continue to innovate and anticipate future threats, — Amir states during a strategic meeting, his serious gaze fixed on Stuxnet's performance data. — The world is evolving, and we must stay ahead to ensure our nation's security.

Covert missions in France and elsewhere have become an essential component of our global strategy, each infiltration a crucial piece of the complex puzzle in our fight against nuclear proliferation. Technical challenges, such as the countermeasures implemented by Iran to detect and neutralize our cyber-attacks, are constant and require rapid adaptation and continuous innovation.

My personal reflections on the evolution of intelligence push me to consider the future implications of cyber operations. The line between defense and aggression becomes increasingly blurred, with each sabotage mission demonstrating our ingenuity and determination, but also raising moral and ethical questions. The quest to neutralize nuclear threats transforms into an inner struggle to maintain a balance between strategic effectiveness and moral integrity.

As I gaze at the twinkling lights of Tel Aviv from my office, I know that our mission is just beginning. Cyberspace is an infinite playground, filled with possibilities and dangers, where every operation is a delicate dance between innovation and responsibility. Mossad, with its cyber arsenal, continues to evolve, ready to face future challenges with the same determination and technological agility that allowed us to triumph in this invisible war.

«Top Secret» Operations from 1948 to Today

Chapter XVII

Behind the Negotiations

The twilight of international diplomacy envelops Tel Aviv in an aura of mystery and palpable tension. In 2012, negotiations over Iran's nuclear program reach their climax, a complex ballet of fragile alliances and silent power plays. At the heart of this storm, Mossad operates in the shadows, weaving information networks and orchestrating subtle strategies that influence global decisions without ever revealing itself.

Sitting in a concealed conference room within the Ministry of Foreign Affairs, I carefully study the faces of the diplomats gathered around the table. The exchanges are muted, words chosen with surgical precision, each phrase weighed like a note in a delicate symphony. David, our deputy director, speaks, his voice resonating with quiet authority.

— The intelligence we've gathered on Iran's nuclear program is crucial to the ongoing negotiations, — he declares, placing an encrypted copy of a report on the table. — It is imperative that we share this data with our allies while maintaining the necessary discretion to avoid compromising our operations.

The internal tensions within Israel are palpable. Some agents express concerns about releasing information, fearing that disclosure could weaken our strategic position. Debates unfold, oscillating between the need for international cooperation and the preservation of our operational autonomy. Amir, our cryptology specialist, underscores the importance of protecting our sources while facilitating effective collaboration.

— We must find a balance between transparency and security, — he asserts, his piercing gaze scanning the room. — Our allies rely on our intelligence to make informed decisions, but we cannot afford to compromise our collection methods.

Secret meetings with foreign diplomats multiply, each interaction a delicate dance between trust and suspicion. The exchanges are often punctuated by heavy silences, with every gesture and glance carrying multiple meanings. One memorable incident occurred during a clandestine meeting in Paris, where a key diplomat inadvertently revealed critical information about Iraq's intentions. The tension escalated, each second a battle to interpret the true intentions behind his carefully chosen words.

— We need to accelerate our efforts, — David murmurs in my ear, his eyes fixed on the diplomat with unwavering intensity. — Every clue can bring us closer to our goal, but we must remain vigilant against potential manipulations.

International negotiations are an arena where alliances form and dissolve in the blink of an eye, and Mossad's role is both influential and invisible. Diplomatic pressures grow increasingly intense, with each country seeking to maximize its interests while navigating an ever-shifting geopolitical landscape. The strategic information we share serves as powerful leverage, shaping discussions and steering the course of negotiations without ever revealing our true hand.

The challenges we face are numerous and complex. The intricacies of international security systems, the need to protect our sources and methods, and the shifting dynamics of international relations require flawless adaptability and ingenuity. Every intelligence-gathering mission is a deep dive into the labyrinth of power and influence, where even the slightest misstep can have global repercussions.

One evening, as I return late from one of these exhausting meetings, I find myself gazing at the glittering lights of Tel Aviv from my office. Personal reflections on Mossad's role in these negotiations overwhelm me. The line between national protection and international interference grows increasingly blurred, with every strategic decision a delicate compromise between effectiveness and ethics. Moral dilemmas accumulate, pushing me to question the legitimacy of our actions and the true nature of our mission.

— We do what's necessary to ensure our nation's security, — Amir confides during a discreet conversation, his words resonating with poignant sincerity. — But it's essential that we remain conscious of the broader implications of our choices on the global stage.

Exchanges with diplomats are often fraught with tension and subtlety, each word a piece of the strategic puzzle we must assemble to achieve our goal. Meetings in Brussels, New York, and London offer opportunities to strengthen alliances, share critical intelligence, and coordinate efforts to curb Iran's nuclear ambitions. However, each interaction is also a test of patience and discretion, where even the smallest lapse can be exploited by our adversaries.

The effects of our actions on Iran's nuclear program are tangible and significant. Subtle sabotage and diplomatic pressure contribute to slowing Iranian progress, sowing confusion and mistrust within their scientific and military teams. However, these successes also come with increased regional tensions, with each victory a provocation for those seeking to upset the established balance of power.

For me, these negotiations represent a dual battle: an external fight against Iran's nuclear ambitions and an internal struggle with my own doubts and questions. The responsibility of sharing sensitive information with our allies while protecting our methods is a heavy burden, with every decision a step toward an uncertain future. Personal reflections on the morality of our actions mingle with an unshakable determination to protect our nation, creating a complex duality that defines my existence as a Mossad agent.

Another memorable incident occurs during a secret meeting in Berlin, where a European diplomat expresses reservations about our approach. The discussions grow tense, the exchanges loaded with innuendo and veiled threats. The ability to maintain our composure and determination in the face of these challenges is crucial, each interaction a test of our resilience and strategic ingenuity.

— We understand your concerns, — David responds diplomatically, his voice calm but firm. — But our objective is to prevent a nuclear catastrophe that would threaten not only Israel but global stability. We must act with determination and solidarity to achieve this shared goal.

The Iranian regime's reactions to the international negotiations are closely monitored. Every move by their diplomats, every public statement, is analyzed for clues about their true intentions and next steps. Mossad, as a strategic force, plays a key role in this analysis, providing valuable intelligence that influences the course of negotiations and global political decisions.

Internal tensions in Israel are also a crucial aspect of this dynamic. Political debates and divergent opinions on how to handle the Iranian threat create an atmosphere of division and distrust, testing the cohesion of our nation and our organization. Mossad, as a secretive entity, must navigate this turbulent landscape carefully, balancing societal expectations with the complex realities of global geopolitics.

For me, these negotiations are a deep immersion into the backstage of power and influence, an experience that enriches my understanding of diplomacy and strategy while reinforcing my determination to protect our nation. Interactions with international experts and high-level diplomats allow me to sharpen my analytical and negotiation skills while confronting the moral and ethical challenges inherent in our mission.

— Every decision we make has far-reaching consequences, — David confides during a late-night meeting, his serious gaze fixed on the analysis reports. — We must remain vigilant and adaptive, anticipating our adversaries' moves while strengthening our alliances with our closest allies.

Internal discussions within Mossad become increasingly frequent, with each agent bringing their own perspectives and concerns about how to manage this complex threat. Debates are intense, with every opinion carefully evaluated to determine the best course of action without compromising our integrity or effectiveness. The ability to work as a team and overcome our differences is essential to maintaining our strategic position and ensuring the success of our missions.

Reflecting on past events and the ongoing negotiations, I realize how critical this period is for our organization and for the future of our nation. Mossad's role in these negotiations is both strategic and invisible, a silent force shaping the course of events without ever revealing itself publicly. The ability to influence international decisions while preserving our operational secrecy is a testament to our ingenuity and our determination to protect our people at all costs.

As the months pass and negotiations continue, the complexity of the Iranian nuclear threat becomes increasingly apparent. Technological challenges, geopolitical dynamics, and internal tensions multiply, but Mossad continues to navigate with unparalleled precision and discretion. The successes of sabotage missions, coupled with strategic intelligence shared with our allies, reinforce our position while underscoring the need to remain constantly vigilant and adaptive in the face of emerging threats.

Another memorable scene unfolds during a secret meeting in Geneva, where a European diplomat expresses concerns about the potential escalation of regional tensions. The discussion becomes intense, with every word a subtle diplomatic maneuver aimed at maintaining balance without triggering an open crisis.

— We must proceed with caution, — the diplomat emphasizes with a hint of skepticism. — Moving too quickly could not only compromise our negotiations but also provoke an uncontrollable reaction from Iran.

David responds with impeccable diplomacy, his words measured and thoughtful.

— We understand your concerns, — he calmly replies. — But Iran doesn't merely threaten our security; they seek to challenge the international order. Our actions are necessary to prevent a nuclear catastrophe that could have devastating repercussions on global stability.

This confrontation highlights the complexity of international negotiations, where every decision must be made with a deep understanding of both strategic and ethical implications. Mossad, as a secretive entity, plays a crucial role in this process, providing intelligence that guides diplomatic decisions while operating in the shadows to neutralize threats before they become uncontrollable.

The internal tensions within Israel are exacerbated by this dynamic, with each agent feeling the pressure to maintain the balance between operational effectiveness and moral integrity. Debates about how to handle the Iranian threat are frequent, with every opinion weighed carefully to determine the best strategy to adopt.

For me, these negotiations represent a deep dive into the backstage of power and influence, an experience that enriches my understanding of diplomacy while reinforcing my determination to protect our nation. Exchanges with international experts and interactions with high-level diplomats allow me to sharpen my strategic analysis and negotiation skills while confronting the moral dilemmas inherent in our mission.

— We must continue to innovate and anticipate Iran's moves, — Amir declares during a strategic meeting, his determined gaze fixed on the data screens. — Every piece of intelligence we share with our allies is another piece of the puzzle that helps us curb their nuclear ambitions.

Secret meetings become key moments where our strategies are refined and adjusted based on new information and developments on the ground. Every intelligence-gathering mission, every sabotage operation, is a crucial piece of this global strategy to neutralize the Iranian threat without triggering an open confrontation.

The technological challenges of this era are considerable. Iran, with its limited but determined resources, has developed sophisticated countermeasures to detect and neutralize our cyber operations. This forces us to constantly innovate and improve our methods, with each success quickly followed by a new phase of development to counter the enemy's new defenses.

Another significant moment occurs during an infiltration mission in Tehran, where our team successfully obtained critical information about Iran's plans to strengthen its nuclear program. The mission, though risky, was a success, providing valuable data that guided international negotiations and the economic sanctions imposed on Iran. However, this success is not without cost, as tension and pressure continue to mount within our team.

— Every successful mission strengthens our determination, but it also increases the risks and responsibilities we bear, — David confides during a debriefing meeting, his serious gaze betraying deep fatigue. — We must stay united and vigilant to continue protecting our nation effectively and ethically.

Personal reflections on the evolution of intelligence and the nature of our mission are constant, with each day bringing new lessons and perspectives. The cyber war, exemplified by operations like Stuxnet, has revolutionized our approach to intelligence and sabotage, but it has also introduced new dimensions of complexity and moral responsibility.

Reflecting on past events and the ongoing negotiations, I realize how crucial this period is for Mossad's future and for our nation's security. The ability to influence international decisions while maintaining our operational secrecy is a testament to our ingenuity and determination to protect our people at all costs.

As I close my eyes and let my thoughts wander, I feel both exhausted and determined. The international negotiations over Iran's nuclear program are a theater where Mossad plays an invisible but decisive role, a strategic force shaping the course of global events without ever revealing itself. The responsibility of sharing sensitive information with our allies while protecting our methods is a heavy burden, with every decision a step toward an uncertain but vital future for our nation.

The challenges faced in this negotiation process are numerous and varied, from managing fluctuating alliances to manipulating information to influence political decisions without ever losing our discretion. Intelligence-gathering missions become increasingly complex, with every operation requiring meticulous planning and flawless execution to avoid any failure that could compromise our strategic position.

In the end, the backstage of international negotiations is a maze of challenges and opportunities, a stage where Mossad continues to play a crucial role in protecting our nation from nuclear threats. The successes and failures of our sabotage missions, coupled with the strategic intelligence shared with our allies, strengthen our position while underscoring the need to remain constantly vigilant and adaptive in the face of emerging threats.

Mossad, with its ingenuity and determination, continues to evolve, ready to face future challenges with the same precision and discretion that have always defined us. As an agent of this legendary organization, I am determined to pursue this mission with the same rigor and passion, knowing that every action taken is another step toward the protection and prosperity of the State of Israel in a world of perpetual change.

Chapter XVIII

Operations in Hostile Territory

The dawn breaks over the Iranian desert, casting the horizon in shades of orange and gold. The dunes stretch endlessly, creating a landscape both majestic and unforgiving. It is in this arid and hostile environment that we conduct our latest missions, each operation a dangerous dance between discretion and audacity. Recent Mossad actions in Iran have redefined our approach, pushing us to the limits of ingenuity and resilience.

Sitting in the underground bunker of our secret base, I pore over the detailed maps spread before me. Every mission is meticulously planned, each detail analyzed with obsessive precision. David, our deputy director, points to a strategic point marked on the map.

— This is where we must intervene, — he states firmly. — The Alvand uranium refinery is operational. If we don't neutralize this facility, the implications for our national security will be disastrous.

The logistical challenges are immense. Transporting

sophisticated equipment across monitored borders requires flawless coordination. Armored vehicles, equipped with cutting-edge technology, navigate treacherous terrain, avoiding enemy patrols via carefully plotted routes. Every kilometer traveled is a test of patience and vigilance, where the slightest mistake could compromise the entire mission. The nights spent under the desert stars are long and silent, punctuated only by the distant hum of turbines and the hot breath of the sandy wind.

One striking memory from this mission remains etched in my mind. In the heart of the refinery, we had to infiltrate a heavily secured building, guarded by armed men and advanced surveillance systems. The tension was palpable, each step echoing like thunder in the oppressive silence of the desert. Amir, our technology expert, skillfully disabled the security cameras, while Yitzhak, our explosives specialist, prepared the charges needed to sabotage the critical infrastructure.

— We only have a ten-minute window, — David whispered, his eyes fixed on the control screens. — Once we're in, we must act quickly and disappear before the alarm is triggered.

The adrenaline surged as we entered the building, our fluid, coordinated movements reflecting months of preparation and intense training. The corridors were narrow and cluttered, creating a maze of dark passages where every shadow could conceal a potential enemy. Suddenly, an explosion reverberated, marking the start of our operation. The lights flickered off briefly, plunging the building into darkness before they blazed back on, revealing the chaos we had unleashed.

The ever-present dangers were not limited to visible enemies. The crushing heat, lack of oxygen, and risk of structural collapse added an additional layer of threat to each mission. Our strategy for operating undercover relied on our ability to anticipate and counter these dangers, using advanced camouflage techniques and secure communication to avoid detection.

Another personal anecdote perfectly illustrates the challenges of these operations. During a mission in Syria, we had to infiltrate a military camp to gather vital information on enemy troop movements. The camp, surrounded by barbed wire and watchtowers, was a stronghold of determined opposition. We used meticulous disguises and forged identities to blend in with the environment, advancing with extreme caution. Every encounter with a guard or officer was a test of nerves and cunning, each decision potentially the difference between success and failure.

— Stay focused, — Yitzhak whispered as we approached the command center. — One mistake and everything collapses.

Missions in hostile territory are trials of mental as much as physical strength. The solitude and uncertainty weigh heavily on our shoulders, each agent confronting their own fears and doubts. Personal reflections on the nature of our mission and the necessary sacrifices become constant companions, fueling a quiet determination to protect our nation at all costs.

During a particularly perilous operation, we were tasked with sabotaging a clandestine laboratory used for chemical weapons development. The site, hidden in rugged mountains, was an impregnable fortress, protected by sophisticated security systems and heavily armed guards. The team had to navigate through narrow tunnels and hidden passages, using jamming devices to neutralize motion sensors and electronic alarms.

— This is where we end this project, — David declared, his tone grave. — We can't allow this to continue.

Executing the mission became a race against time, every second a battle against exhaustion. The explosive charges were placed with meticulous precision, each movement a demonstration of our expertise and determination. Once the sabotage was complete, we had to disappear as quickly as we had arrived, evading enemy patrols and the traps set by enraged guards.

The impact of these operations on the geopolitical balance is both significant and profound. Each successful sabotage weakens our enemies' military capabilities, slows their weapons programs, and sends a clear message of our determination to protect our nation. However, these actions also heighten regional tensions, each victory perceived as a provocation by those seeking to overturn the established order.

For me, personal involvement in these missions is a source of adrenaline and satisfaction, but also of reflection and questioning. The realistic and dangerous nature of our operations pushes me to my own limits, forcing me to develop the resilience and ingenuity essential for survival and success in such hostile environments. Moments of extreme tension, where every decision counts and where every mistake can be costly, are trials that forge our character and strengthen our resolve.

— We must always stay one step ahead, — Amir declared during a post-mission debriefing. — Iran will never stop looking for ways to increase its power. We must anticipate their moves and remain vigilant.

The strategies for operating undercover constantly evolve, adapting to new technologies and enemy defense methods. The use of reconnaissance drones, encrypted communication systems, and advanced camouflage devices has become routine, with each innovation integrated into our missions to maximize effectiveness and minimize risks. Collaboration with technology and cybersecurity experts is essential, each operation requiring a perfect synergy of skills and expertise from our team.

One particularly memorable mission took place deep in Tehran, where we had to infiltrate a ballistic missile launch base. The site, located in an isolated valley and surrounded by mountains, was protected by a formidable military force and advanced surveillance systems. The team had to navigate narrow paths and hidden tunnels, using jamming devices to disable radars and motion detectors.

— We must neutralize these installations without alerting enemy forces, — David declared, his determined gaze fixed on the map. — This is our only chance to prevent an imminent attack.

The operation was a demonstration of our expertise and ability to operate in the most hostile environments. The explosive charges were placed with millimeter precision, each detonation calculated to maximize impact on the military installations without triggering a violent response. Once the sabotage was complete, we had to disappear quickly and quietly, avoiding Iranian army patrols and the traps set by vigilant guards.

The impact of these operations is immediate and tangible. Iran's military installations are severely damaged, slowing their ability to deploy ballistic weapons and maintain their military superiority in the region. However, these successes also lead to increased regional tensions, with each victory seen as a provocation by those seeking to upset the balance of power.

For me, these missions in hostile territory are a source of intense adrenaline and personal satisfaction, but they are also marked by a keen awareness of the risks and necessary sacrifices. The brutal reality of modern warfare, where discretion and precision are paramount, is a constant lesson in the limits of our power and the need to remain vigilant in the face of emerging threats.

Chapter XIX

The Weight of Secrecy

Dusk gently falls over Tel Aviv, casting the city in a golden glow that contrasts with the inner darkness I feel. Life as a Mossad agent is shaped by secrecy, where each day is a silent struggle between duty and personal desire. On this quiet evening, I find myself alone in my office, memories of past missions swirling in my mind like the distant shimmering lights of the city. Living a secret life has demanded immense sacrifices. Hours spent away from family, missed encounters with friends, and moments of intimacy sacrificed for dangerous missions have left invisible scars I carry with me. Each successful operation is a professional victory, but it leaves behind a personal void that is hard to fill. Smiles shared with loved ones have been replaced by forced smiles and heavy silences filled with unspoken truths.

Personal relationships have become complex puzzles. My loved ones sometimes feel an inexplicable distance, a subtle absence that is not always easy to explain. Questions about my frequent absences are often diplomatically dodged, but the truth is harder to conceal. The distrust and confusion others feel toward my mysterious behavior are constant reminders of the price I pay to protect my nation. The solitude of an agent is a silent companion, with each successful mission strengthening my commitment but also deepening my isolation. The psychological weight of secrecy is a heavy burden. Memories of risky missions, constant dangers, and life-or-death decisions haunt my nights. Each failed operation or mistake leaves an indelible mark on my mind, feeding silent doubts and deep regrets. The line between right and wrong becomes increasingly blurred, with each action becoming a matter of national survival but also a personal moral trial.

I remember one particularly poignant mission where the line between duty and humanity vanished. In the midst of a sabotage operation, I had to make a quick decision to save my teammates at the expense of innocent people accidentally caught in the crossfire. The stifled cries and terrified faces of the victims are etched in my memory, a brutal reminder of the unforeseen consequences of our actions. This experience forced me to reconsider the nature of our struggle, where every tactical victory comes with a personal loss. Deep reflections on this secret life push me to seek a fragile balance between duty and personal redemption. Every day, I question whether the sacrifices made are truly worth it, whether the price paid is justified. The conviction to protect our nation remains unshaken, but it is often tested by the inevitable moral dilemmas that arise. The question of whether we can justify our actions in the name of national security is a constant internal battle, a struggle that tears at my soul.

The powerful memories of these years of service are both a source of pride and pain. Moments of camaraderie with my colleagues, tactical successes, and small personal victories are precious memories that illuminate the darkness of our secret existence. However, these memories are often tinged with regret and loss, reminding me of the lives sacrificed and the missed opportunities due to our unwavering commitment to the mission. My personal involvement in each operation has shaped who I am today. The resilience and determination developed over the course of the missions have taken root within me, making me stronger but also more vulnerable to the inner turmoil the job inflicts. The ability to remain calm and focused in the face of danger has become second nature, but it has also created a certain emotional distance, a protective barrier against the psychological wounds that come with the territory.

A poignant memory comes to mind from after an especially grueling mission, when I found myself gazing at the stars in the desert, searching for answers in the vastness of the night sky. The silent beauty of the stars contrasted with the inner chaos I felt, a search for meaning in a life dominated by uncertainty and risk. That moment of solitary reflection reminded me of why I chose this path but also of the personal costs it entails. Relationships affected by this secret life have become fractures that are hard to heal. Family and friendships are often strained, with each absence and necessary lie to protect our secret widening the gap between me and those I love. Reunions are fraught with unspoken tension, fleeting glances, and superficial conversations that fail to bridge the emotional distance created by our double life. The difficulty in maintaining authentic relationships is a silent pain that accompanies every success and failure. The weight of secrecy has also impacted how I perceive myself and my role in the world. The duality between the dedicated agent and the individual seeking redemption creates a constant inner conflict, a struggle to find meaning in a life dictated by clandestinity and danger. Reflections on justice and vengeance intermingle, with each mission a quest for national protection but also an exploration of the limits of our own humanity.

Ultimately, this secret life has shaped who I am in an indelible way. The sacrifices made, the relationships affected, and the psychological weight of secrecy have forged a complex identity, marked by unwavering determination but also deep emotional vulnerability. The constant pursuit of national security has become an integral part of my being, a personal mission that transcends external challenges to become an ongoing internal struggle. As I gaze at the moon's reflection on my office wall, I realize that this life of secrecy and sacrifice is a double-edged sword—a force that drives me to protect my nation while costing me dearly on a personal level. Solitude and moral dilemmas are inevitable companions, but they are also constant reminders of the complexity of our mission and the sacrifices necessary to ensure the survival and prosperity of the State of Israel. Contemplating the distant lights of Tel Aviv, I feel both proud and weighed down by the burden of secrecy. This life as a Mossad agent is a quest for justice and protection, but it is also a personal struggle against the sacrifices and losses that come with it. The road is long and fraught with challenges, but the conviction to protect our nation remains my guide, despite the silent burden I carry each day.

The Secret History of Mossad

Chapter XX

A Mossad Agent's Confession

Dusk slowly settles over Tel Aviv, coloring the sky with orange hues that gradually blend into the emerging darkness. Sitting in the quiet of my office, I take a moment to reflect on everything this career has brought me. It is not a formal conclusion but rather a personal introspection about the path traveled, the sacrifices made, and the lessons learned as a Mossad agent.

The years spent in this secret organization have been a series of intense and formative experiences. Every mission, whether it was successful or marked by challenges, contributed to shaping my character and worldview. I learned that true strength lies in resilience and the ability to stay focused even in the most perilous situations. Determination and perseverance became my loyal allies, allowing me to overcome the constant obstacles and unforeseen challenges that arose along the way. One particular anecdote remains etched in my memory. During a mission in hostile territory, we had to infiltrate an Iranian nuclear facility. The tension was palpable, every move had to be calculated with millimeter precision. We navigated through narrow corridors, avoiding enemy patrols with impeccable coordination. At a critical moment, a silent alarm went off, signaling a possible intrusion. Thanks to our calmness and ingenuity, we managed to neutralize the threat without raising suspicion, but that moment reminded me how every decision could have irreversible consequences.

The personal sacrifices have often weighed heavily on my shoulders. The hours spent away from my family, the missed gatherings with friends, and the moments of intimacy sacrificed for dangerous missions have created fractures in my personal relationships. The loneliness of a Mossad agent is a silent companion, with every successful mission strengthening my commitment but also deepening my isolation. However, these sacrifices have also reinforced my belief that our mission is essential for the safety and prosperity of our nation. The psychological weight of secrecy is a heavy burden to carry. The memories of risky missions, the omnipresent dangers, and the life-or-death decisions haunt my nights. Every failed operation or mistake leaves an indelible mark on my mind, fueling silent doubts and deep remorse. The line between right and wrong becomes increasingly blurred, with every action dictated by national duty but also by a conscience tormented by the human consequences of our choices.

As I gaze at the stars in the night sky, I recall moments of solitary reflection, searching for answers in the vastness of the universe. These moments of introspective calm have become essential to finding balance between duty and the pursuit of personal redemption. The quest for justice and the protection of our nation collided with the harsh reality of human lives, creating a dissonance between professional duty and personal guilt. Personal relationships have often been strained by the clandestine nature of our work. Frequent absences, necessary lies, and constant pressure have created insurmountable distances with my loved ones. Reunions are fraught with unspoken tensions, evasive glances, and superficial conversations that fail to conceal the depth of the emotional chasm created by our double life. The difficulty of maintaining genuine relationships is a silent pain that accompanies every success and every failure.

This life of secrecy and sacrifice has forged a complex identity, marked by unwavering determination but also by deep emotional vulnerability. The relentless pursuit of national security has become an integral part of my being, a personal mission that transcends external challenges to become a constant inner struggle. The sacrifices made, the affected relationships, and the psychological weight of secrecy have shaped a resilient and determined identity, ready to face the uncertainties of the future with hard-earned wisdom. By sharing these reflections, I hope to offer the reader a window into the soul of a Mossad agent, a deep understanding of the sacrifices and dilemmas that shape our existence. For beyond the operations and missions, it is humanity and the search for meaning that truly define our journey, constantly reminding us why we do what we do and at what cost.

As I look at the twinkling lights of Tel Aviv from my office, I know that my journey within Mossad is an integral part of who I have become. The memories, sacrifices, and lessons learned will continue to guide my steps, even far from missions and secret operations. This life as an agent, with all its challenges and rewards, has forged a resilient and determined identity, ready to face the uncertainties of the future with wisdom gained at a high price. The path I have traveled is marked by successes and regrets, but each step has been an essential part of building my understanding of justice, loyalty, and the protection of our nation.

«Top Secret» Operations from 1948 to Today

Printed in Dunstable, United Kingdom

David **Haddad**

The Secret
History of
Mossad

REVOLU

Révolu SAS, 91 rue du Faubourg-Saint-Honoré, 75008 Paris cedex, France

The Secret History of Mossad